UNHINGED

ROGER L. CONLEE

Pale Horse Books

ISBN: 978-1-939917-51-5

Other historical novels by Roger L. Conlee:

EVERY SHAPE, EVERY SHADOW
COUNTERCLOCKWISE
THE HINDENBURG LETTER
SOULS ON THE WIND
FOG AND DARKNESS
DARE THE DEVIL
DEEP WATER
AFTER THE WIND
LION AT TWILIGHT

www.PaleHorseBooks.com
www.RogerLConlee.com

All are available through PaleHorseBooks.com, as well as Amazon and Barnes & Noble.

www.palehorsebooks.com
www.RogerLConlee.com

UNHINGED

ROGER L. CONLEE

Pale Horse Books

ONE

I'd just finished having lunch with Mack Sennett, the creator of the Keystone Kops, at the Brown Derby in L.A. I was working on a documentary about the slapstick comedies of the 1910s and '20s. It was a wonderful day—*until it wasn't*. Not after that gunshot was fired.

Mack Sennett was seventy-four years old here in 1954 and had been out of the movie business for years, but he remained an engaging guy with a solid, retentive memory. Still a novice at TV, I was the West Coast correspondent for CBS.

We had chatted about the Army-McCarthy hearings in Washington, debunking his claims about Soviet agents burrowing into our government like termites. I had done a story on how dangerous to our democracy the chronic liar Senator Joseph McCarthy was, and had received death threats in return.

But we didn't dwell on that; mostly we talked about his Keystone Studios' rivalry with Hal Roach back in the day. As I took notes for my documentary, I sensed Mack had some lingering bitterness toward Roach, but actually very little.

We discussed some of the stars he'd had under contract, including a young Gloria Swanson, W.C. Fields, the tragic Roscoe "Fatty" Arbuckle, and the lovely Mabel Normand, who starred with Charlie Chaplin in many of his films. Sennett had been especially pleased that he'd first teamed Normand and Chaplin in a film in 1914. It was all very open and cordial. We made plans to meet again about my documentary.

Bob Cobb, owner of the Brown Derby and the inventor of the Cobb Salad, or so he claimed, came by and held court with us for a while. Cobb was also part owner of the Hollywood Stars baseball team. He told us they'd be pretty good this year.

Now leaving the restaurant, Sennett and I stepped out onto the Wilshire Boulevard sidewalk under an April sunshine that glittered on the concrete like silver coins. He was taller than me and had a good, firm stride for an older guy. Cars whirred by on Wilshire.

We turned onto Alexandria Avenue, heading for the Derby's parking lot in the rear.

Three or four pedestrians were headed our way. Suddenly, one of them pulled out a handgun. And fired at us!

Sennett was hit. I was right next to him. Blood spattered on my jacket. Sennett went down like a felled tree.

"Stop that woman," I screamed. "Stop that woman!" I was pretty sure the shooter was a woman.

TWO

I knelt down to see what I could do for Sennett. He'd been hit in the side, the side that was closest to me. I'd been inches from being shot myself.

"Run into the Derby and call for an ambulance," I shouted at a boy who'd materialized behind us, gawking at the scene.

Sennett's eyes were open. He groaned. I put a hand on the wound in his side and felt bone. Jagged bone. The shot must have broken a rib. Blood oozed through my fingers.

"Hold on, you big Canuck," I said. (He'd been born in Canada.) "We'll get you to the hospital and fixed up." *I hoped.* I pulled open his suit jacket, took a hanky from my back pocket and held it against the wound. I knew if I could slow the bleeding, even a little, it would help.

People crowded around. "Somebody get a cop," a voice bellowed.

"Did anybody catch that woman?" I demanded, not looking up from Sennett.

"What woman?" someone said.

It felt like an hour later, but was probably only five minutes when a siren howled and an ambulance squealed to the curb. Mount Sinai Hospital was written on its white doors. Young men jumped out and took over from me, placing an oxygen mask on Sennett's face, pressing some kind of a large, white pad on his wound, then gingerly lifting him onto a gurney and sliding it into the rear.

A cop had turned up. He asked me a ton of questions. Yes, my name was Jake Weaver. I worked for CBS. The man who was just rushed away was Mack Sennett, the famous silent-movie producer. We'd been having lunch. Yes, I think the shooter was a woman. No, I didn't get a good look at her, I was focused immediately on Mack Sennett. Flowery jacket, pink scarf, I think. When someone's pointing a gun at you, you're looking more at the gun than the person.

The shooter, whoever she or he was, was long gone.

The cop said a detective would call on me that afternoon for follow-up.

THREE

I'd been the network's West Coast correspondent for about half a year after a long career as reporter and editor at the *Herald-Express*. CBS had considered me and Everett Hensley, a reporter for NBC Channel 4. Fortunately they picked me over Hensley.

Not long ago I'd made a trip to West Germany on behalf of Great Britain's MI6, a hush-hush deal. On my return I did my warning piece on Joseph McCarthy, saying the senator was lying and dangerous when he called nuclear scientist J. Robert Oppenheimer a communist. After that, I made the decision that a documentary on the old-time kings of comedy would be a good change of pace for me.

I drove back to Columbia Square, our studios on

Sunset Boulevard. We shared the building with our affiliate station KNX while the futuristic CBS Television City was being constructed out at Fairfax and Beverly. It would be another couple of years before that massive edifice was up and running.

In my third-floor office, I hung my topper on my antique hat stand and peeled off my suit jacket, looking at the splatters of blood on it. There were a few on my pants, too. Dry cleaners, here I come. The office contained my oak desk, three chairs, a two-line telephone, and a 12-inch Dumont TV set with rabbit-ear antennas. Framed photos of my wife Valerie and daughter Ilse sat on the desk. Valerie had lush brunette hair and the deepest blue eyes; Ilse's hair was rusty brown like my own.

Just outside my office a smaller room was home to my middle-aged secretary, Betsy Morgan, and my intern, Bambi Scott, a journalism student and senior at USC.

I knew Mack Sennett wasn't married and lived alone in Woodland Hills. I called a towing company I'd used before and made arrangements for his car to be hauled there from the Brown Derby parking lot and the bill to be sent here.

Next I called Mount Sinai but couldn't learn anything about Mack's condition. He was in surgery.

They'd know more later.

I was pretty shook up. It's not every day you come close to getting shot. I wanted to talk with my wife Valerie. Hers was always a good shoulder to lean on, if even figuratively.

But first things first. I called in my intern and said, "Bambi, please take down these words and get them to the network office for tonight's crawl," the crawl being the news flash that was supposed to scroll across the bottom of the screen. It was still experimental and didn't always work. Before she got out her notebook Bambi saw the blood on my jacket and gushed, "What happened, Mr. Weaver?"

After I told her, she said, "Oh my God, it must've been scary. How close was it?"

I put one hand on my hip and the other a short distance away, estimating. "Around ten inches I guess. Too darn close, Bambi. Now take this down: 'Old hyphen Time Hollywood Comedy Producer Shot in L.A. Bang.'"

"Bang?" she asked, puzzled. "That doesn't sound right."

"Bang is newspaper shorthand for an exclamation point," I explained. "It saves time when a reporter in the field calls dictation to the rewrite desk. I want the crawl to end with an exclamation point."

She wrinkled her elegant nose and said, "I get it. Bang. I like it." She scribbled away, then handed me her notebook so I could proof what she'd written. OLD-TIME HOLLYWOOD COMEDY PRODUCER SHOT IN L.A.!

"That's it, thanks," I said. "Get this over to the news room."

With a "For you, Mr. Weaver, anything," off she went, twitching her comely behind at me, deliberately I thought. Well-named, the lissome and frisky, 21-year-old Bambi was forever flirting with me. She *was* pretty. I thought she also had the makings of being a good journalist some day. She lived with girlfriends in a sorority house near the campus. I appreciated that she was solicitous. Her concern about my close call felt genuine.

I called our network anchorman Douglas Edwards in New York and filled him in. "Thanks, Jake," he said, "I didn't even know Mack Sennett was still alive. Give me three minutes worth for our 6 o'clocker. I'm sure we can find a photo of the guy."

I had always been a reporter of the news, not part of the news itself, but that was about to change. Our local outlet learned of the shooting from their police scanner, and KNX reporter Jerry Dunphy came to see me. After all, shooting one of the old kings of comedy was news.

I insisted on just an audio interview, no film—I didn't need my mug on TV—and told Dunphy all I could. I insisted he play up Sennett and not the fact that a CBS correspondent was almost shot. The story would lead the night's local news.

After Dunphy left, Miss Morgan showed in the detective who'd been promised. It turned out to be a guy I knew, Owen Wannamaker. We'd dealt with each other at least twice before.

After shaking hands, I waved him toward a chair facing my desk and said, "Good to see you, Owen. What's it been now, a couple of years?" His brown eyes were almost the same color as my fedora.

"Yeah, since you and Bela Lugosi walked in on that dead lawyer. Strange case, that one." Wannamaker pulled a notebook and pen from his jacket pocket and said, "I see some blood on your coat there. Mack Sennett's blood, they tell me. You sure get into some strange stuff, Weaver. Tell me about it."

I told Wannamaker I was starting to do a documentary on the silent slapstick comedy days, focusing on the Mack Sennett-Hal Roach rivalry. I'd had preliminary interviews with each man, who were older now but still alive and kicking.

"How come you wanta do that?" he asked.

"There's been a revival of interest now that a lot of those old films have been released to television. Reruns of Laurel and Hardy and the Our Gang comedies, stuff like that, are damn popular at the moment."

"Yeah, I've seen some of those myself. Funny stuff."

"Owen, I've had one interview with Sennett at his house and today we had lunch at the Derby, our second session together. Only one interview with Roach so far."

Wannamaker jotted something in his notebook, looked up and said, "So, as I understand it, you and Sennett were leaving the Derby, heading around the corner toward their parking lot and somebody coming toward you up and plugs the guy, is that it, Jake?"

"Right. I think it was a woman, bright-colored jacket, short skirt maybe, but I didn't get a close look 'cause I ducked by instinct, then real quick turned to Sennett. I held a hanky to his wound till the ambulance showed up. I shouted for somebody to stop her or him but I guess nobody did. Man, I hope Mack makes it."

"So do I. Our patrolman at the scene said nobody tried to stop the shooter. Too scared to try an' go after somebody carrying a gun. A couple of our uniforms questioned witnesses and the kid you had call an ambulance, but got nothing. Questioned people in the surrounding streets, too. Nada! They didn't find a bullet or a shell casing. You said they were rivals. You figure Hal Roach is behind this?"

"Don't know, Owen, but I doubt it. That rivalry's been over a couple of decades now and when I talk to these guys I don't sense any real bitterness. These guys used to raid each other for talent, and people have long memories. I have no idea who'd want to kill Mack Sennett, but somebody sure as hell does so you guys ought to put a guard on his hospital room."

"We already have, Weaver. Give us some credit."

Wannamaker got up, put away his notebook and handed me a card. "I figure you know how to reach me, Jake, but just in case. Call if you think of anything else. This case'll probably be mine, so you'll likely be seeing me again."

Wannamaker left.

I rolled my chair over to the teleprinter, next to the wall. The machine had a keyboard like a typewriter and was linked to most of our affiliates but more importantly to our HQ in New York. I began to bang out my "three minutes" for Douglas Edwards, which I knew meant 300 to 350 words.

No sooner had I finished than my old friend Marko Janicek from the *Herald-Express* showed up. "Who's that little blond honey you got in the outer office?" the reporter asked with a worldly smirk. I told him that was Bambi Scott, a college student part-timer here.

Marko gave me a "you dog, you" look, glanced out the window at the traffic on Sunset Boulevard, and then settled in the visitor chair. He tossed his gray felt hat on the desk, and got out his notebook. A native Serbian and an ex-U.S. Army Ranger, Marko had an L-shaped scar on his left cheek, a souvenir of the war.

I went through the whole thing again. Marko was a good reporter and I knew he'd write a solid piece that would go out on Hearst's wire, the International News Service.

"Almost getting shot is a frightening thing," said Marko. "I know. I got hit on the cliffs above Utah Beach on D-Day and again a couple weeks later at Rouxeville, plus more near misses than I could count. I hope you're holding up okay."

"I got shot at myself during the war," I said, "in Berlin." I closed my eyes and for a moment I was seeing it again. Rolf Becker, a German newsman I thought I knew and trusted sneaks into my apartment at night and fires at me. The shot misses my face by a whisper. Its heat stings my left ear and cheek. I've seen and felt this scene over and over. It plays in my sleep sometimes. Too many sometimes. I also sometimes have a nightmare about a Joseph McCarthy hitman coming after me.

"Hey, Jake, you okay?"

I opened my eyes. "Yeah, Marko, I'm okay." To be honest, I was still pretty not okay. But I went ahead and answered all his questions.

"Who do you think did this and why?" he asked.

"I don't know but I'm going to find out. That's off the record, pardner, my trying to find out. Don't want the cops to think I'm doing a parallel investigation, gettin' in their way."

"You've still got some Louisiana in your voice, don't you," Marko said.

"Reckon maybe I always will."

"Was the change from newspapers to TV very tough?" he asked.

"Not so much, but I'm uneasy about being on camera, Marko. I prefer being behind the scenes."

Before he closed his notebook and left I asked how the old gang at the *Herald-Express* was doing. Aggie Underwood, Jack Campbell, Frank Fisk and the rest.

After Janicek came the *Times* and then the *Examiner*. Hell, I could have made a recording of the previous interview answers and played it for them while I took a nap.

I was tired and wrung out by the time all their questions were answered. I called Mount Sinai and learned that Sennett was out of surgery and resting. His condition was listed as "serious to critical." I heaved a sigh of relief that he was still alive. I figured that serious to critical was better than plain critical, but not a whole lot better.

FOUR

I needed to talk to my clever wife Valerie. I called her at Lockheed, where she worked in rocket development, one of the few females in the country to do that. Man, I was proud of that gifted woman. She had silky black hair and blue eyes I could drown in. Valerie was in conference with some other engineers, though, and unavailable. Darn, I'd have to tell her about it later at home.

I kept an old pair of canvas pants in the office to wear when a story took me to the desert, a junkyard, or someplace out in the boonies. I put them on and on my way home I brought my suit pants and jacket to the dry cleaners we used. The guy there, Luigi, looked at the blood spatters, frowned and said with a shake of his head, "We weel do our best, Meester Weaver."

It was my night to provide dinner—we took turns. I was far too done in to prepare a meal so I stopped at a joint we liked called the Purple Dragon for Chinese takeout. Beef with broccoli, fried shrimp, vegetarian egg rolls and steamed rice.

On reaching our home on Saturn Avenue, I found Valerie had just arrived and was uncorking a bottle of pinot noir. After a warm hug and kiss, she said, "Hey Sailor, what's with the old pants?" She often called me Sailor, knowing I'd had a hitch in the Navy before my newspaper days. "What happened to the clothes you went to work in?"

"They're at the dry cleaners. They've got some blood on them, Mack Sennett's blood."

"What? Let me pour this wine, then let's sit down and hear about *that*."

After telling her what happened, she said, "Do you think there's any connection between the shooting and you working on this documentary?"

"I doubt it, Val. I've only just started and the only people who really know about it are Sennett and Hal Roach, plus my bosses at the network. Seems to me if Roach wanted to kill Sennett he would've done it years ago, back in the twenties when their rivalry was hot, not now that they're old men. I know what Roach looks like and the shooter sure didn't resemble him. Like I said, it might even have been a woman."

"You couldn't tell?" she asked, those azure eyes probing mine.

"Nope. It happened so fast. When Sennett was hit I went down to my knees in a flash. When somebody's shooting at you, you duck! But there's a vague picture in my mind of a woman's pink scarf. I could be wrong, though. It was all so fast."

Valerie took a sip of wine and said, "Sennett and Roach were enemies back in the silent movie days?"

"I wouldn't say enemies, Sweets, but certainly adversaries." I sometimes called her Sweets. She liked that. "They would raid each other's studio for talent, but there's no record of any violence, at least not that I've found yet."

"Well, I'm sure glad the shot didn't hit you. It was close, right?"

"Damn close, Val. I was really unnerved for the next hour or two. Mostly okay now."

"You've always been good at perseverance, Sailor."

"How did your day go, Val? Better than mine, I hope."

"We had a long, tiring conference on ways to improve the thrust chamber on the Viking 8, which we're developing in cooperation with the Glenn Martin

Company. The first seven Vikings were similar to the German V-2, but the Eight is wider, taller and requires more thrust." Valerie sighed. "I could go on but I don't feel like rehashing all that tonight."

Being one of the few women in rocket development, she worked almost exclusively with men. If she had any notions of a brief indiscretion she'd have plenty of candidates to choose from. But I was confident she had no such notions. We were very much in love.

"Hey, it's time for the news," I said, jumping up and clicking on our new Zenith TV. Tuned it to Channel 2. "Let's see what Doug Edwards did with my story."

A guy standing at a bathroom mirror told us that with Brylcreem a little dab would do ya.

Then came our logo, the "CBS Eye," leading into the Evening News. Edwards opened with an airliner crash in Turkey that killed twenty-five people. Our story came up third. "In Los Angeles today, an old-time producer of silent slapstick comedies was shot and seriously wounded in broad daylight just outside a popular restaurant. Mack Sennett, who was known for the Keystone Kops, W.C. Fields and other stars of that era, tonight is in critical condition in a hospital there."

A face shot of Sennett appeared, then a few seconds of Keystone Kops footage, as Edwards went on to say the gunman or woman was at large, and there was no known motive for the shooting. The crawl worked, creeping across the bottom of the screen just as we'd hoped, ending with a bang. Edwards closed with, "Ironically, our West Coast correspondent Jake Weaver was with Sennett when he was shot. He had been interviewing him for a possible story. Weaver stayed with the wounded Sennett till an ambulance crew arrived."

Valerie, who'd been looking closely at her watch, said, "Three minutes and 32 seconds."

"He asked me for three minutes," I said. "Doug gave us a tad more than that. Adding that mention of me, he wandered from what I wrote. I don't want to be part of the story but I guess I am to some extent."

When a pretty actress in high heels started telling us that no other washing product could get our clothes as clean as Oxydol, Valerie clicked off the TV and said, "C'mon, let's dig into this Chinese feast you brought us. I'm famished."

Later that night, she helped to ease my stress in that special way she had.

FIVE

Back at the office next morning, I called Mount Sinai to check on Sennett and ask if I could see him. He was doing well, considering, his condition now listed as serious, not critical. And no, I couldn't come see him for at least another day.

At least he was going to live. Thank God for that. I then called Hal Roach at his studios in Culver City to see if I could meet with him again, either there or at his home in Bel Air. We'd met once before when I'd just started on the documentary project.

"We're knocking off early here today," he said, "waiting for some new lighting equipment that won't arrive till tomorrow. I never turn down CBS so come out to the house if you want, around 2:30. But I'll tell you up front I had nothin' at all to do with shooting Mack. He's like a brother to me."

"That was a white lie. Roach respected Mack Sennett, no doubt, but wouldn't call him a brother.

 "I know," I said. "Thanks, Hal, and I'll see you this afternoon."

Roach had lasted longer in the business than Sennett had. In fact, he was still going strong at age 62, turning out movie shorts and films for TV.

Born in Elmira, New York, he'd been a cattle wrangler and a gold prospector before coming to California in 1913 and meeting comedian Harold Lloyd.

The Hal Roach Studio he started the next year eventually boasted the incomparable Laurel and Hardy, the Our Gang comedies and later the popular humorist Will Rogers. Unlike Sennett, he'd transitioned into talkies successfully when sound came to the movies.

His 1937 comedy *Topper* starring Roland Young and Constance Bennett made a star out of a relative newcomer named Cary Grant. This film, one of Roach's biggest successes in the thirties, proved to be the springboard to Grant's great career.

The Sennett-Roach rivalry had been intense. Sitting at my desk, chewing on a yellow pencil, I asked myself: Could Hal Roach or someone on his behalf have tried to kill Mack Sennett yesterday, decades after his movie career was dead and buried? I didn't think it likely. There were hard feelings, but it seemed to me that if one of them had reached such a level of anger that he actually wanted to kill the other, that point would have been reached in the 1930s, not now, some twenty years later.

I knew both men. Liked them. Didn't think they harbored murderous intent.

I then thought about Roach's dubious deal in 1937 with Vittorio Mussolini, son of the Italian dictator. The idea was that Roach would produce a series of films trumpeting Italian culture, starting with an adaptation of *Rigoletto,* with the goal of boosting the reputation of daddy's Fascist regime. The trouble was that Benito Mussolini had invaded Ethiopia and signed an alliance with Adolf Hitler the year before and his popularity in the U.S. had taken a nosedive.

I made a mental note to bring that up with Roach this afternoon.

SIX

On my drive to Bel Air, with Country KXLA on my radio, my fingers were tapping on the steering wheel to Kitty Wells singing "It Wasn't God Who Made Honky Tonk Angels."

I found Hal's home and parked in its circular driveway. The place was a curious fusion of architectural styles. The timbered left half of the front comprised two stories, while the adjacent right half stood one story, stuccoed, with pillars in front, a gabled roof and two chimneys jutting up. One of the halves must have been an add-on sometime after the original was built. The place was big but not as ostentatious as many in the movie community. Harold Lloyd's Greenacres Estate was twice as large. As I got out of my Chevy Deluxe, a wide garage door was open and I could see the big headlights of a maroon-colored Deusenberg. My daughter Ilse would love that car.

I went to the front door, which was in the right front. Before I could touch the bell the door opened and there stood Lucille Prin Roach, Hal's wife. I'd learned that she had been a secretary in Ohio when they'd met during the war, Hal being stationed nearby in the Army, producing training and propaganda films. They'd been married about ten years.

"You must be Mr. Weaver," she said. "Please come in. I enjoyed the report you did on how Fredric March and Donald O'Connor co-hosted the Oscars from different places." She was a brunette with an oval face anchored by a delicate nose and blue-green eyes. Not beautiful, but pretty. I thought her husky voice, which reminded me of Peggy Lee's, was kind of sexy.

"Thanks very much, Mrs. Roach."

"Now now, Mr. Weaver, please call me Lucille."

"All right then, and I'm Jake."

"It's certainly a shame about poor Mack Sennett," she said, stepping backward into the room to let me enter. "I do hope he'll be all right. Do you have any new information?"

"It looks like he'll make it, Lucille. His condition is serious but not critical."

At that moment Hal Roach burst into the room. Big and burly with a broad face, he looked like he could be a rugby player in his green, short-sleeve shirt. He wore denim pants, cowboy boots, had a ready grin and looked younger than his 62 years. Born in Ireland, he still had the gift of gab.

"Hey there, Jake, I see you've met my Lucille. We usually have a guy here answering the door but it's his day off. Come on back." He gestured for me to follow him into a large sitting room with a stone fireplace. Picture windows spilled feathery sunlight across a plush carpet.

Roach took a seat on a beige wing chair and I settled opposite him on a luxuriant sofa of the same color. Through the windows loomed a huge backyard. I couldn't see it from where I sat, but I was sure there must be a big swimming pool out there.

I got out my notebook and said, "I want to ask you mostly about your early movie days for my documentary, but—"

"But you want to know," he jumped in, "if I have any idea who might've shot Mack, and I sure as hell don't. It damn sure wasn't me. I have an airtight alibi. I was at the studio at the time with at least a dozen witnesses. Seems to me if someone was sore at him over one of those ancient scandals he would've done something back then."

I figured he was referring to the tragic Fatty Arbuckle affair and the William Desmond Taylor murder in the 1920s.

"I see it that way, too," I said. Those scandals hurt Sennett, even though he personally had nothing to do with them. "Moving along then, let me ask about the Vittorio Mussolini business."

A reluctant frown crossed Roach's face. He got out a cigarette and offered me one, a stalling technique. As I didn't smoke, I declined. He lit a match with his thumbnail, fired up his smoke and said, "I was afraid you'd bring that up. Well, you see, Vittorio came to me, back in '37 it was. He was an affable guy, gregarious, and we had a few drinks. He told me how much he liked American movies. Then he made his proposal. I kind of liked the idea of making a few films with him about Italian culture. We set up a joint venture called RAM—Roach and Mussolini—and started in on the first project.

"Dumb me. I didn't think about how Italy had invaded Ethiopia, was blackballed by the League of Nations, and how papa Il Duce had cozied up with Hitler. The Hollywood rags got hold of it, I got labeled a Fascist-lover, and MGM killed the distribution deal I had with them. I had to buy my way back into that. I can tell you, MGM cost me a pretty penny. Jake, don't ever do business with Louis B. Mayer! After I shut down RAM, Vittorio slunk back to Rome, and that was that."

Roach snuffed out his cigarette in a crystal ashtray. "Before long, the whole thing smoothed over. Fortunately, the public sometimes has a short memory. By the way, Vittorio survived the war and now he's operating some Italian restaurants in Argentina, of all places."

"And with *Topper* you got back some of the money you lost to MGM," I said. "Am I right?"

"That you are, Jake. Cary Grant was terrific. Casting him with Constance Bennett in that film did wonders for his career—and my bank account. The way that pair teased old Roland Young didn't need much directing."

"How did you get along with Constance Bennett?" I asked, recalling that slinky blonde.

Roach gave me that locker-room gaze and coy smile men often have when telling tales out of school. He glanced around to see if Lucille was nearby. "You see, I wasn't married at the time."

I figured we'd gone down that road far enough, so I turned to some of his stars from the silent days.

"Finding Laurel and Hardy was the greatest piece of luck I ever had," he said, smacking a right fist triumphantly into his open left hand. Stan Laurel was born in England, you know. He'd been working for me as a writer but I knew he was from a theatrical family and had some vaudeville experience, so in 1921 I think it was, I teamed him with big Oliver Hardy in a comedy short. The result was magic. I made 'em big stars in no time. Wait, that's not fair. They made *themselves* big stars. Those fellas are comic geniuses. And they made a smooth switch from silent films to the talkies. Good comic voices."

Lucille came in at that point, carrying a tray and saying, "It's time you boys had a little snack." She'd brought coffee and cookies. "Fresh brewed and fresh baked," she said. "Homemade."

Biting into a peanut-butter cookie I told her it was yummy and could she show my wife Valerie how to bake. Val, bless her heart, was a good cook but not a culinary artist.

After Lucille left, I put down my coffee cup and picked up my notebook. "Laurel is a little guy, right?" I asked.

"Not really. He's average height, but he looks small next to Hardy, who's six-one and goes about 280. Those oldtimers are still at it. They're touring England right now and drawing huge audiences. NBC has approached me about doing a big special on those guys."

"NBC?" I uttered, feigning hurt. "Why not CBS?"

"Sorry, sport, but you guys didn't come to the party. It's NBC's idea."

We talked a bit longer, bringing up Charlie Chaplin and Will Rogers. Then he changed the subject, saying, "You really lit into Joseph McCarthy the other day. Nice going."

McCarthy, the far-right nut case from Wisconsin, had been claiming that J. Robert Oppenheimer, the father of the atomic bomb, was a communist because he'd opposed development of the more powerful hydrogen bomb. Maybe he felt guilty about the A-bomb or maybe he thought, Why build a bigger one if we already had a weapon that could destroy an entire city and kill thousands of people? It would be beyond overkill.

I'd produced a piece saying it was just wrong for McCarthy to make such public statements without any proof. Irresponsible character assassination.

"That clown deserved it," Roach said. "Let's hope these hearings with the Army will shut him up."

Shortly after that I thanked him for his time, and asked if we could borrow some Laurel and Hardy footage for my project. No problem, he said. I told Lucille how nice it was to meet her, how good her cookies were, and took my leave.

Driving away, I reflected on how much more

successful Roach had been in his later years than Sennett, whose film career had petered out some years ago.

And why in hell would someone want to kill him?

I thought about Roach's Mussolini fiasco. Wondered if Sennett had been one of the many who openly condemned Roach for that. Could there be an Italian connection?

Edward R. Murrow had done a CBS report on how Il Duce's surviving family members were doing. After the war, Vittorio Mussolini became a film critic before emigrating to Argentina and setting up his string of restaurants. Could Vittorio harbor a grudge against Mack Sennett on behalf of his old friend Hal Roach? Enough to hire a hit man? Or hit woman?

SEVEN

Back at the office Betsy Morgan fetched my notebooks for me and I reviewed what I had so far. Bambi brought me coffee with her usual flirtatious grin, which was starting to get old. I said, "Thanks, darlin' " and she replied, "You've got a bit of Southern accent, don't you, sir?"

"I reckon. Was born in Loozanna and my first news job was in East Texas so I guess some of that way of talkin' rubbed off on me. Now it's late afternoon, Sugar, so take the rest of the day off."

She left and I turned my thoughts to the scandals of the 1920s and about Vittorio Mussolini. In the 1920s and '30s his Papa Benito had virtually wiped out the Mafia, or so he claimed. I'd been told that in actuality, though, the Mafia just laid low in Italy and let Il Duce enjoy his bluster while concentrating their criminal activities in the States.

If Daddy had been anti-Mafia, could his son have been the opposite and ordered an underworld hit on Mack Sennett? Maybe I'd ask my gangster contact Mickey Cohen about that.

More or less the mob's man out here in L.A., Cohen ran the numbers racket and most of the hookers, too. He was close to Lucky Luciano and Meyer Lansky in New York.

Cohen had become a source for me during my newspaper days and he seemed to like being a pal to what he considered a big-time journalist and fellow boxer. He had boxed professionally in the '30s (winning eight and losing eight) and I had been a pretty good amateur middleweight in the Navy.

Mickey Cohen could wait. I'd concentrate on the scandals, the biggest of which was the Roscoe "Fatty" Arbuckle affair in September of 1921. The jovial, amusing Arbuckle had become a big comic star after signing with Sennett's Keystone Studios in 1913.

Eight years later he threw a lavish Labor Day weekend party at the St. Francis Hotel in San Francisco, inviting several of his friends, friends of both genders. Among them was the model-actress Virginia Rappe, a lovely and canny 30-year-old brunette.

She had co-starred with Arbuckle in the 1917 film *His Wedding Night,* and had also appeared with newcomer Rudolf Valentino in a film that didn't do much. Rappe was a notoriously loose woman who had slept her way into the movies. She'd undergone more than one abortion and a baby she'd had in 1919 with producer Henry Lehrman had been placed in foster care.

The party went on for three days of boozing, sex and drugs. At the end of the first day, Virginia Rappe complained of convulsions. On the second day she was howling with severe abdominal pain. On the morning of the third day she was found dead of a ruptured bladder.

The media got hold of it: sensational story! It was immediately speculated that Arbuckle's 300 pounds had crushed her while having sex. Many of the revelers, though, claimed that Fatty hadn't made love to Rappe, and that she'd complained of abdominal pain from the very first day.

Fatty was tried for manslaughter three times. The first two trials ended in hung juries and in the third he was acquitted. There was no concrete evidence and the defense claimed that Rappe's many abortions probably had created an abdominal precondition. Nevertheless, the scandal ruined Arbuckle. He limped along in minor parts for a few years and directed some inferior shorts but his star was forever tarnished. Fatty Arbuckle was through.

I tried to think of any possible connection between that scandal and the shooting of Mack Sennett. Mack had had nothing whatever to do with the party and had even urged Arbuckle not to go to San Francisco over the holiday because they were in the middle of shooting a film.

Arbuckle had been Sennett's boy but I couldn't see how anyone could blame Mack for what happened at the St. Francis and bear a grudge over that for three decades.

EIGHT

In the morning I called Mount Sinai and learned that I still couldn't see Mack for another day. He was better but still weak. I'd gotten wind of a rumor that this hospital might merge with Cedars of Lebanon to form Cedars-Sinai Medical Center. Not a bad idea. I thought both were first-rate.

So I drove down to my old haunt, the *Herald-Express* on South Trenton Street, close to the Electric Railway's trolley barns. I planned to do some research in their morgue, newspaper speak for library. First I went to the city room where my old compadres gathered around for some how-ya-doings. They all knew I'd almost been shot; Marko Janicek's story had clued them on that. I was glad to see that the publisher,

William Randolph Hearst Jr., wasn't around. I didn't like the man. He was the reason I'd left newspapering for TV.

I told city editor Aggie Underwood that I'd like to do some poking around in the morgue. She readily agreed on condition that I'd have a drink with her afterward in the Continental, the saloon across the street. How could I not agree to that with the first female city editor in the country and a great friend to boot? Many called her a "great broad," about which Aggie didn't complain.

I was still focusing on the old Hollywood scandals so in the morgue I looked for clips from the 1920s about the William Desmond Taylor murder. The 49-year-old Taylor had directed some forty films, including a few with "America's Sweetheart," Mary Pickford. In film circles it was said the sophisticated, English-born Taylor gave Sennett's Keystone Studios some class.

But on the night of February 1, 1922, he was murdered in his Alvarado Courts apartment, shot in the neck and shoulder. The last person to see him alive was Mabel Normand, the Keystone actress and Mack Sennett's former lover. She claimed she'd dropped by to borrow a couple of books. It was rumored that she and Taylor had also been lovers, such was Hollywood in those days, young actors intoxicated by sudden fame and playing musical beds.

Mabel Normand said Taylor had been deeply worried about the disappearance of his secretary after forging checks and about having to bail out his butler from jail for soliciting young boys.

There were plenty of suspects in Taylor's murder, including Normand, a woman named Mary Miles Minter, another of Taylor's lovers, and even Minter's mother, who was said to be enraged because he'd deflowered her daughter. Sennett himself was also quizzed by police as a possible suspect. In the end, the L.A. cops remained baffled and no one was ever charged.

Then came the strangest twist of all. A screenwriter couldn't make up this stuff. The victim wasn't Williams Desmond Taylor at all, but a guy named William Cunningham Deanne-Tanner. Never born in England, Deanne-Tanner had been an itinerant actor, a prospector in the Yukon, and an antiques dealer in New York. He'd deserted his wife in 1908, gone to L.A. and reinvented himself as William Desmond Taylor.

The *Herald-Express* headlines were lurid and black. Hearst always went for sensationalism.

"Jesus!" I said as I scribbled most of this in my notebook. It was no wonder that the Catholic Church screamed to high heaven and the Production Code came into being. I wondered how any of this cockamamie, sordid Desmond Taylor business might tie in to a murder attempt on Sennett thirty years later. I couldn't see it.

Soon I was sitting at the bar in the Continental, the newspaper hangout across the street, with Aggie Underwood. Photos taken over the years by news photogs, some of them autographed, covered the walls. Ballplayers, boxers, actors, politicians, strippers from the burlesque joints. Shaker, my longtime bartender pal who now co-owned the place, greeted us with "Pretty low company you're keeping there today, Aggie." Then he grinned and gave me a big handshake. "Whatever you're having is on me," he said. "Great to see you, ya big TV star. Falstaff?" he asked, mentioning my usual beer.

"Nope, make it Early Times and water, light on the water, pardner." Beer wouldn't do it after my Taylor murder findings.

"Heavy stuff today, huh, Jakey?"

Aggie said she'd have her usual vodka martini. After the drinks arrived, she wanted to know what I'd found.

I told her about my notes on William Desmond Taylor, who wasn't even William Desmond Taylor at all. "Man, Hollywood was out of control in the '20s, wasn't it?"

"I was a little girl at the time, Jake, but I remember some of it. My folks were captivated by all that stuff. It almost ruined Sennett. He continued on, getting Gloria Swanson, W.C. Fields and some other big names, but he'd lost his swagger. Still had some good years but Hal Roach was beginning to leave him in the dust by the late '20s."

"I knew the Hearst papers always go for the sensational," I said, "but back then they were even more yellow than today, weren't they? Can I have a photographer shoot a few of those garish front pages with the big banner heads about Arbuckle and Taylor for my documentary? We'll credit the *Herald-Express*, of course."

"Sure thing," Aggie agreed.

After talking about old Hollywood a bit more, I asked how things were at the paper now that Hearst Junior was in charge.

"Oh, you know, not bad I guess. Fortunately, he doesn't come in every day. Nobody likes him the way we liked W.R." Meaning the late William Randolph Hearst. "It's rumored that Junior might merge us with the *Examiner*." That was Hearst's morning paper in town. "If he does that, my ass is outta here. Probably high time I retired anyway. But I'll tell you this, Jake. We miss you."

As I was leaving, Shaker, wiping a glass with a towel, said, "Get your butt in here more often, Jake." He put the towel down and we slapped hands.

Driving away from that old south-side neighborhood I had a warm, good feeling. Talking with first-rate newspaper people like Aggie Underwood did that for you.

NINE

That same nightmare crept into my bed and took hold of me that night. I saw the flash of the gun muzzle light up the darkness of the room and felt the bullet zip past close to my ear, stinging my face. My subconscious told me that somehow one night that bullet wouldn't miss and that would be all she wrote. Any future I might have, permanently eradicated. Lights out.

I woke up in a sweat, hoping I hadn't disturbed Valerie, but I had.

"Hey Jake," she whispered. "It's all right." She reached over and placed a gentle hand on my forehead. Then she kissed my cheek.

"Thanks, Sweets," I murmured. I stared at the murky ceiling for a long while hoping that movie wouldn't play again tonight. At last I fell back to sleep.

But only for an hour or so, when the room seemed to tremble. It felt as if the bed quivered a little. Earthquake, I thought. Had felt them before.

Over breakfast in the morning, I asked Valerie if she'd felt the earthquake.

"Earthquake? No, I didn't, Jake. Did you?"

"Yeah, I'm pretty sure there was one. The room felt unsteady for a moment or two, like you were in a boat." We turned on the radio and after a commercial—Gillette Super-Speeds gave the smoothest shaves ever—heard about what was being called the San Jacinto Earthquake. It was centered eighty to ninety miles east of here, doing considerable damage in Palm Springs and San Bernardino. Even knocked some plaster off the walls at L.A.'s City Hall.

"CBS will need a story," I said. "When I get to the office I'll call Doug Edwards and see how much they want. I'll try to get some footage at City Hall and maybe other places around town where there might be some damage."

"Sounds good," Valerie said, "but tell me more about those scandals you researched yesterday. That's fascinating stuff."

I rehashed some of the Fatty Arbuckle and James Desmond Taylor affairs, and then said, "Have I mentioned Mabel Normand? She was a star in those early days and Mack Sennett's lover for a while. Everybody expected them to get married but they never did. I'll have to ask Mack about that, if he recovers enough to talk some more, that is. Well, a year or so after the Desmond Taylor thing Normand's chauffeur was found standing over a murdered L.A. millionaire named Cortland Dines. He was holding a pistol belonging to Mabel Normand. More huge black headlines. Normand never really recovered from the Desmond Taylor and Cortland Dines double tragedies, and she died at age 36. We don't seem to have scandals like that anymore."

"We don't?" Valerie said skeptically. "How about Errol Flynn caught bedding those under-age girls? And Clark Gable getting Loretta Young pregnant when he was married to someone else?"

"You're right, Val. I forgot about those. I guess fame and infamy, fed by bloated egos, will always go hand in hand. Must be human nature." I finished off my toast, put down my coffee cup and said, "Guess I'd better get off to work. It'll do me good to think about an earthquake, something other than Mack Sennett for a while."

Valerie kissed me and said, "And I'm off to rocketland."

And that's what I did that morning. Called our San Bernardino station and the cops in that town, also their hospital, and jotted down a lot of details. Also checked with the cops in Palm Springs. I tracked down a seismologist at UCLA, who said the San Andreas Fault was "a continental right-lateral strike-slip transform." It was the state's most dangerous fault and passed beneath San Bernardino. That was more than I wanted to know but "most dangerous" and "beneath San Bernardino" were two items I'd use in my story.

I sent a cameraman over to City Hall to shoot some footage of the cracked plaster and to scout around in town for other damage he could film. He found some in a Woolworth's and a Cut-Rate Drugs.

New York wanted all the film we could give them and four minutes of script. I'd been able to supply that by 11:30. Bambi had classes that morning, which was a good thing. I could crank out my work without her looking over my shoulder, asking questions and could she fetch me some coffee. The gal was often a big help but she could also be a bother.

In fact, my secretary Betsy Morgan, a widow of

about fifty, told me a couple of times that Bambi, while a smart one, was a flirt and that I should keep on my guard.

My earthquake chores completed, I called Mount Sinai Hospital and learned that Mack Sennett was awake intermittently and his condition had been upgraded from critical to serious. I could visit him if I kept it brief.

I grabbed some lunch at Clifton's Cafeteria on Olive Street, ham sandwich on rye, cup of mushroom soup, and a Pepsi. And then it was off to the hospital.

Before going up to Sennett's room I tracked down his surgeon, a Doctor Groves. Found him eating a salad in the doctors' lounge/cafeteria. He had gray eyes, a narrow face, thinning brown hair, and looked to be in his late forties. After introducing myself, he said, "Sure, Weaver, have a seat. I remember your byline. One of the *Herald*'s hotshots, aren't you?"

"Not anymore, sir, I'm with CBS now, their West Coast guy. I'm doing a documentary on old-time movies. I'd been interviewing Sennett and I was the man next to him when he was shot."

"Good golly, Weaver. You're fortunate to be alive. You pressed a handkerchief to the wound until the paramedics arrived, I understand."

"That's right."

"Damn good move, Weaver. That helped."

"Seemed like the thing to do, doctor. What can you tell me about his wound and his chances?"

Groves finished a bite of broccoli, put down his fork, and said, "The bullet cut through two ribs on his right side and ripped a piece out of his stomach. Luckily it passed just below the lung and above the large intestine. I've seen a number of gunshot wounds and I'd say this was caused by something larger than a .22 caliber bullet, possibly a .38. I went in and stitched up his stomach. The procedure took about two hours. He's now thoroughly bandaged on that side and we're medicating him for pain. We have to watch and make sure my sutures on his stomach wall hold and he doesn't bleed there. He was in pretty good shape for a man of his age. He'll survive and die of something other than this, years from now."

I hadn't been taking notes. I could remember all that. I'd learned that people will talk more openly if you aren't jotting down their words in front of them. "Thanks, doc."

"Surely, Weaver. Now, who do you suppose might have done this? Who would want to kill Mr. Sennett?"

"That's the sixty-four dollar question. If the cops don't find out, I will. How long will he be hospitalized?"

"It depends on how fast he recovers, but for at least

a week. We've got to make sure the stomach is healing and there's no infection."

"Thanks, Doctor Groves. Okay if I go see him?"

"Yes, but don't stay too long. He needs his rest."

As I got up to leave he stuck out his hand and I shook it. I liked the guy.

TEN

I walked in and found Mack lying in bed, eyes closed, looking about as pale as the white blankets that covered him. A breathing tube ran from his nose to a canister beside the bed and another tube snaked from his left arm to an IV drip stand from which dangled a bag of fluid.

I approached almost tiptoeing and sat in the visitor chair by the bed. "Mack," I said softly. "Mack, can you hear me?"

He opened his eyes, glanced the wrong way, then refocused in my direction. "Hey there," he uttered in little more than a whisper. "They say I'm going to live a little longer."

"I've been talking to the doc," I said. "He tells me

you're a tough hombre and are gonna make it just fine." After a beat I went on. "Do you remember what happened after we left the restaurant the other day?"

"My memory's pretty screwed up. Don't recall much of anything after . . ." He paused and took a breath, then another. ". . . you and I were walking to the parking lot. Just that some people were coming toward us and one of them pulled out a, a, a gun. Nothing after that."

A nurse came in at that moment. White smock, gray hair, grandmotherly. She laid a hand on Mack's forehead, seeing about fever I guess, and then checked the level in the drip bottle. "Don't stay long, sir," she told me.

I said I wouldn't and then she was gone.

"With your stomach healing up from a gunshot wound, what can you eat?" I asked.

"Just some kinda weak soup. Guess I also get some nutrients through that tube there." Again, it was little more than a gravelly whisper.

"You'll be eating juicy steaks again before long," I said. "Say, I had your car towed to your house."

"Thanks. Forgot all about my car."

"Listen, do you recall what the person with the gun looked like? Could it have been a woman?" I asked.

"Couldn't say. Can't remember. It's all a fog."

"Mack, can you think of anyone who'd want to kill

you?"

He scrunched his forehead and said, "Mabel Normand for sure, if she was still alive." He allowed himself a small chuckle, then grimaced as if that hurt him. "You see, Mabel and I lived together for years, we were a couple." He paused to catch a breath before continuing. "But I always chickened out when she wanted to get married. I hurt her and I damn sure regret it. Why in hell didn't I marry her? Best woman I ever knew. Worst mistake I ever made." I could see the pain in his face as he thought back. "When she left me she was furious. She coulda done it back then, Jake, killed me. Oh, yeah." Another pause for breath. "But Mabel's been dead more'n twenty years. Can't think of anyone else."

The nurse returned, glared at me and said, "Really, sir! You and that detective Wannamaker."

I got to my feet and winked at her, which only made her glare more. Now I knew that Wannamaker had been questioning him too. Looking back at the patient, I said, "Mack, you're in good hands. You rest up and get well. I'll see you again in a few days."

He gave me a weak grin and I was gone.

* * *

On the way home, I stopped at the dry cleaners and picked up the pants and jacket I'd been wearing when Mack was shot. The pants were totally clean but there was a tiny dark spot on the jacket that Luigi hadn't been able to eliminate. He apologized but I said no need, I knew he'd done his best.

It was Friday night so Valerie and I went out to dinner. Let someone else cook for us, we agreed. Deciding to try something new, Valerie suggested the Smoke House in the valley, not far from Lockheed, her place of work. She hadn't been there but had heard good things about the place from co-workers.

The Smoke House turned out to be practically across the street from the Warner Brothers studio. The exterior was faux English Tudor. Inside, we found scores of red leatherette booths, similar to what they had at Musso & Frank's. The lacquered-wood walls were covered with photographs of stars, mostly from Warners, I thought. The place was crowded; a good thing we'd called for reservations.

We were led to a booth and I ordered a bottle of cabinet sauvignon. "Which winery and vintage, sir?" the waiter asked. I hadn't even peeked at the wine list. "You choose," I said. "Pick a good one."

After fluffing her napkin and placing it in her lap, Valerie glanced around the room and said, "I think that's Virginia Mayo about four tables over. Don't recognize the man she's with."

I looked and said, "I think you're right. I didn't realize she had red hair. Usually looks more blonde in the movies." I'd met Miss Mayo at a big dinner party William Randolph Hearst threw at San Simeon nine or ten years ago. Don't recall her hair color at the time.

"She's an attractive woman," Valerie said.

"Without a gown, heels or fancy hairdo in *Along the Great Divide*, a Western with Kirk Douglas and Walter Brennan, she was prettier than in any of her other pictures I've seen. Her natural beauty came through."

"You're quite the connoisseur of pretty women, aren't you?"

"Damn right," I said. "And I landed the prettiest of them all."

"You're so full of it," she said but I knew she liked getting compliments like that.

We picked up our menus. The wine arrived a few moments later. The steward showed me a bottle, saying, "Inglenook, 1949. I think you might like this."

I motioned for him to open it, which he did with a practiced flourish, then poured a small amount into a glass for me to taste. I swirled my glass, sniffed and sipped, gave it my okay, and he poured for both of us, left the bottle and departed.

I lifted my glass to Valerie and said, "To the world's prettiest rocket engineer."

She clinked her glass against mine and replied, "I repeat, you're full of it."

When the waiter came by, Valerie ordered the veal and I asked for the filet mignon, medium rare. We both asked for garlic bread and Caesar salads.

"Speaking of pretty women," Valerie said, "how's that cute little intern of yours?"

"How do you know she's pretty?" I asked.

"Because when I ask how she looks you talk about her journalistic instincts or something instead of answering the question." Man, you couldn't beat Valerie for savvy.

After our meals were served, we talked about the Mack Sennett shooting, my daughter Ilse, who'd just returned from Germany, and what we would do tomorrow. Being Saturday, we'd both have the day off.

"Why don't we do something completely different?" Valerie said.

"Good idea," I agreed. After a moment's thought, I said, "How about the Pike in Long Beach? We could ride the rides, take in the funhouse, have hotdogs and cotton candy, and bum around like a couple of teenagers."

"You're on," Valerie said, "except for the cotton

candy. I haven't been to that amusement park in ages." She set her fork down, looked off to her left and said, "That fellow a couple of tables over looks a bit like Ray Dudley."

I glanced that way, saw a rather nondescript guy with brown hair, and asked, "And who is Ray Dudley?"

"Back in Illinois, he was a close friend of my late husband Jim. He was kind of sweet on me."

"I can't blame him," I said. "You're a very desirable woman." I tried to give her an alluring Tyrone Power gaze but probably failed.

"Oh, come on," she demurred. "But as to Ray, he thought he could get somewhere with me, but I wasn't interested. A: I was in mourning, and B: He wasn't my type. He was irritating. Ray got angry when I moved to California. The last I heard he was in pre-med at the U of Illinois. Anyway, the guy over there bears some resemblance but he's not Ray Dudley."

I knew other men had been interested in my wife. It was inevitable, the way of the world. I knew she'd been approached by guys at North American Aviation when she worked there, and now again at Lockheed. The youthful beauty she had when we met twelve years ago had blossomed into a mature and striking elegance. I was humbled that she chose me over the Ray Dudleys out there.

"You look kind of wistful, Jake," she said. "Is your filet okay?"

"Yes, it's great. Want a bite?"

"No, the garlic bread and this excellent veal are filling me up."

The conversation turned to Ilse. My daughter had a small role in a film Leni Riefenstahl had made in Berlin. Riefenstahl, a once-acclaimed director and cinematographer, was now trying to resuscitate her career after being blackballed for making pre-war films for the Nazis.

Ilse was now back at her reporter job at the Pasadena *Star-News*. "She really enjoyed working with Leni Riefenstahl," I said. "I hope she's not thinking about becoming an actress."

"Why not, Jake?"

"Hollywood can be a cesspool, especially for young women. A lot of those movie moguls just use 'em and abuse 'em. I know she's a strong gal, but I'd hate to see her go in that direction."

"Your opinion may be influenced by these scandals you've been researching, Jake, don't you think? Fatty Arbuckle and all that?"

"That's probably part of it, Val."

I knew Ilse had gone to San Diego at least twice since returning from Germany to visit our friends Kenny and

Claudia Nielsen. I had coauthored a book about World War II with Nielsen, a Marine Corps lieutenant colonel and war hero who was now teaching history at a high school down there. Our book, *Two Men at War: A Retrospective*, had done pretty well.

His wife Claudia, a former Navy nurse, had earned her M.D. at UCLA and completed a residency at St. Mary's Hospital in Long Beach before starting her practice in San Diego.

"I wonder why Ilse has gone to see them so often recently," Valerie said.

"I don't know, Val. Claudia was her roommate their last year at UCLA and they got pretty close, and she's fond of Kenny."

"Definitely fond of Kenny," Valerie said. "I've noticed some vibes there."

"Really? I know Kenny and Claudia had a few rough times while she was in med school, but I thought they were doing fine now, her a fledgling physician and him a high school teacher. I sure don't want my daughter getting into something that's none of her business." This was something I'd have to think about.

After finishing our meals, we declined dessert and headed for home.

ELEVEN

We had a light breakfast the next morning, just coffee and cantaloupe slices, saving room for the junk food we knew we'd have at the Pike in Long Beach.

I drove us to the amusement park in my 1950 Chevrolet Deluxe. Taking the straight shot down Vermont for a few miles to Sepulveda, then jogging over to Long Beach Boulevard, we reached the place in just over half an hour.

"Wow, this hasn't changed much over the years," Valerie said after we bought our tickets, and strolled onto the broad midway. There was the old Ferris wheel, the garish sideshow huts, the food vendors, and way in back close to the ocean stood the Cyclone Racer.

Purported to be the only double roller coaster in the world, it featured side-by-side tracks. The cars started at the same time and would "race." The one with the most or the heaviest passengers usually won.

"I'm glad we're doing this," Valerie said, looking around and taking in all the sights. "It's a great change of pace for us."

"Damn right," I agreed. I hadn't thought about Mack Sennett all morning.

First we rode the Ferris wheel. Holding my hand as we neared the top the first time, Valerie said, "Don't rock the car." I had no intention of rocking the car.

"The Ferris wheel" I said, "was invented by a guy from our friend Kenny Nielsen's hometown, Galesburg, Illinois."

"I know," Valerie said. "Gale Ferris. You've told me that many times."

"Repetitious old me," I apologized, sort of.

Next it was off to the Cyclone Racer. I bought our tickets and we got in line along with several people, most of them younger than us. Many were teenagers.

When we got into our seats, a worker lowered the bar in front of us and latched it in place. We were in our car's third row. After the cars on both tracks were loaded, we started the slow climb to the top of the highest hill, where the race would begin. Our "enemy" car was on our left. *Ratcheta ratcheta ratcheta* went the cog wheels as they hoisted us slowly up the track.

Finally reaching the top, we paused for a moment and then over we went, plunging downhill. The kids in front of us raised their arms and screamed. So did people in the car opposite. A little kid in that car stuck out his tongue at us.

Down we plummeted, then up, my gut feeling it. Ugh. And down again. The tracks parted ways as we neared the ocean and for a while we couldn't see the car we were racing. On we hurtled. For a second it looked as if we were out over the water. After two more ups and downs, the tracks drew close again and there were our adversaries, right off to our left. Damn, they were half a car length ahead of us.

At last we rolled onto the final down slope, approaching the level area near the finish. Our team, including Valerie and me, urged our car on with shouts of "Go, go!" It was in vain. We ended up losing, still half a car length behind. The folks in that car hooted at us and a kid in ours called out, "You cheated!" as we all disembarked.

"That was fun," Valerie said, "but I think my stomach got left behind."

"I hope you can find it, because hotdogs and peanuts lay ahead."

Strolling back up the midway, holding hands, we came to a hut with a sign above it that read LIVING ODDITIES, STRANGE PEOPLE. A barker insisted that we just had to come in and see the freak show. We didn't.

Farther along, a swarthy-looking guy without a shirt was bending backward and lowering a sword into his mouth. "Eew," Valerie said, turning her head away. "How does he do that?"

The peanuts lost out, but we did stop at a stand to buy hotdogs and Cokes. After loading up the dogs with mustard, relish and onions, we took seats on a bench to have our meal. The hotdogs hit the spot. Valerie gestured at a sign that said CRAIZY MAIZE and said, "That's the house of mirrors. Let's try that before we leave."

And so we did. You went in there and stood before wacky mirrors that distorted your body this way and that. In front of one, Valerie put her thumbs in her ears and waggled her fingers at her shimmering self. I couldn't help but laugh. Her face was quivering and bloated, looking five times its natural size. Other mirrors shrank our bodies down to midget size, others made us grossly fat, others ten feet tall and thin as pencils. In front of one mirror I stuck out my tongue and it became a giant sausage.

Suddenly this wasn't fun anymore. It was too much. A needle of panic stabbed at me. Mirrors everywhere. Surrounded by cold slabs of glass changing me from one grotesque image to another. Taunting me. I grew dizzy. I had to get away from these mirrors, to escape, but somehow I couldn't. I'd lost my bearings in a sea of cruel, sadistic reflections. I turned this way and that, legs wobbly. Now bullets were being fired from those hellish mirrors. *Bullets.*

"Where's the . . . ?" I screamed, or thought I did. I was lost in there, totally disoriented, trapped, couldn't find the exit. "Help me!"

We were outside in the sunshine, seated on a bench, Valerie holding my hand. "You're okay now, Jake, you're okay. Just rest here and relax a while. What happened in there?"

"Those mirrors were trying to kill me, Val. They were laughing at me and firing guns, big bullets, streaming right at me. I know it doesn't make any sense, but it felt like in another few seconds I'd have been shot to pieces. Maybe by one of Joe McCarthy's disciples. Thank God you hauled me out of there."

She put an arm around me and lightly brushed my hair like a mother soothing a frightened child. My queasy stomach began churning around down there, threatening to push up the remains of the hotdog and make me vomit right here in public. I put a hand on my gut and willed that stuff to stay put. Thank God it did.

Were passers-by giving us strange looks? I didn't know, didn't care.

TWELVE

I'm driving," Valerie insisted when we reached the car. "You've just had a panic attack and Doctor Valerie prescribes rest for you in the front passenger seat."

I didn't argue. The passenger seat would be safe harbor after that soul-shaking experience. I'd had nightmares about almost getting shot but today some fun-house mirrors had given me a "daymare." Craizy Maize indeed!

I relaxed in my seat and watched the scenery go by. A horde of oil wells pumping away on Signal Hill, the Veterans Stadium on Lakewood Boulevard, an Alpha Beta grocery, numerous shops and restaurants.

Valerie was a good driver. I thanked her for driving and said being chauffeured around felt good for a change. She reached over and patted my thigh.

We decided to go to a movie that afternoon. We hadn't been to the movies in quite a while. After checking the listings in the paper, we settled on *20,000 Leagues Under the Sea* at the Oriental Theatre on Sunset Boulevard. Still thinking I might be a little wobbly—I wasn't—Valerie did the driving again. The panic attack was long gone and I was feeling my old self again.

We settled into our seats and watched a Bugs Bunny cartoon, the Warner-Pathé newsreel and previews of coming attractions. The newsreel featured President Eisenhower authorizing an Air Force Academy to be built in Colorado, and Sugar Ray Robinson training for a comeback after being retired from boxing for a couple of years.

Then came the feature and we enjoyed it. Afterward, Valerie and I agreed that James Mason was excellent as the brilliant but off-kilter Captain Nemo.

"Jules Verne had quite a far-seeing mind," I said. "Imagine, writing about a submarine a century before there *were* any submarines."

We lazed around the house that evening. While simply having sandwiches for supper, I said, "I know we ought to take it easy again tomorrow, but I think I'll go see Mickey Cohen for a while, if he's available on Sunday. Won't take long, maybe an hour or so."

"You old war horse," Valerie responded, "you're itching to get back to work, to see if he's got some idea about who shot Mack Sennett, aren't you?"

"You know me too well," I said.

We had both morning papers delivered to our house, the *Times* and the *Examiner*. The Sunday *Times* carried a follow-up story on the shooting. They said Sennett's condition was improving, that he was expected to survive, and that the police still had no leads. Detective Sergeant Wannamaker was quoted as saying they would keep working the investigation. Thankfully, there was no mention of me having been a witness walking alongside Sennett at the time of the shooting.

Mickey Cohen and I usually met at Musso & Frank's Grill on Hollywood Boulevard but when I called he said he needed a change of pace and suggested the Tam O'Shanter.

I found a parking space on Los Feliz Boulevard near that old Scottish steakhouse. The headwaiter said Mr. Cohen was already there and led me to his booth where I greeted him with, "Hey, pardner."

I plopped down across from him. "Good to see

you, Jakester," Mickey said, reaching out for my hand. "After all the crapola I been goin' through, it'll do me good for a change ta talk to somebody from the real world, an old friend who's straight."

A waiter appeared and Mickey ordered a Jack—meaning Jack Daniel's—and I asked for Early Times and a splash of water.

Spencer Tracy walked by just then and Mickey called out, "Hey there, Spence."

"There's a pair to draw to," the actor said as he ambled on by.

Our drinks arrived. Mickey lifted his glass and said, "Bottoms up!"

"Bottoms up!" I agreed and we clinked glasses. After taking his first swig, he lit a cigarette and knew not to offer one to non-smoker me.

A wistful, rather sad look came over his face. "You know, Jake, we shoulda boxed back in the day, at least once. Nothin' serious, just a few rounds. I woulda took pleasure in beatin' ya."

Challenging words I couldn't resist. "Come on, Mick, you went eight and eight. I looked you up. And I was the middleweight champ of the 6th Naval District. You woulda been overmatched."

"The hell! Eight and eight ain't bad against the jigs and beaners I was fightin'. Hungry young pros, tough and fast on their feet. You had it easier'n I did, just facin' amateurs. Anyhow, back then we shoulda strapped on the gloves. Too late now, I guess. Us old farts are gettin' even older." I couldn't disagree with that.

The waiter reappeared and we ordered. Filet mignon medium rare for Mickey and Scottish salmon for me.

I took a taste of my whisky and asked, "How's it going, Mick, really?" I was concerned. It was easy to see he was troubled.

"You know, I'm often gettin' shaked down by greedy cops with their hands out, guys who think I'm not payin' 'em enough to look the other way. Plus, I've had two or three attempts on my life. And then there's punks like Jack Dragna tryin' to cut in on my action. Shit like that I can handle, though it's a pain in the ass. Now, though, I may be in a real jam. This Kefauver Committee's been lookin' close at my taxes. I mean *real* close." I knew about the new Congressional committee headed by Tennessee Senator Estes Kefauver investigating mobsters.

"I got pretty good guys workin' my books," he went on, "makin' my income look all legit, though of course it ain't quite." Deep lines furrowed his brow. "Kefauver could get my ass on tax evasion. That's how they got Capone, ya know, tax evasion. I could do time, Jake. Serious time."

He snuffed out his cigarette in a ceramic ashtray. "Imagine, a man of my religious persuasion, one of the guys Hitler never got his hands on, goin' up the river."

This was the first time I'd ever heard Cohen allude to the fact that he was Jewish, which of course I was aware of. It was also the first time I'd seen him this worried. We'd done each other some favors over the years, but there was nothing I could do to help him on this.

"When this hits the papers, is there some way you could soft pedal it a little? Picture me as a small businessman unfairly hassled?"

I started to say I couldn't possibly, I had my journalistic ethics, but he spoke first.

"Nah, course you couldn't. Sorry, stupid of me. Forget I even asked."

Our meals arrived and conversation lagged as we dug in. Mm, the first bite of the salmon was good.

"Hey, I hear your coauthor buddy, the Marine Corps hero, is in San Diego now," Mickey said after taking a bite or two.

"Right, Kenny Nielsen. He's teaching high school and his wife, a newly minted doctor, has opened up her medical practice down there."

"Hope they don't run into Frank Bompensiero. He's the mob's top man in Dago. Vicious son of a bitch.

One of Jack Dragna's boys. Runs a racetrack wire and hookers, owns a coupla bars, different other stuff down there. Well, you didn't come here to hear about my woes or San Diego scumbags. What's goin' on in your world, Jake? Anything I can do for ya?"

"Well, Mick, at the moment I'm trying to figure out who shot Mack Sennett and why."

"You and the cops both," he said.

"Was the mob involved in any way?" I asked uneasily. "Maybe a hit attempt that missed?"

"You sure as hell should know I don't do hits!" he said with some heat. I hadn't meant to offend him. "I've had some people roughed up once in a while when they needed it, but I never once had somebody whacked. Never once!" I wasn't so sure about that but kept my mouth shut.

"As to others in my field, I ain't sayin'. But as far as I know, Sennett never got sideways with nobody in the business." He took another gulp from his glass. "Now, lemme ask you something. Who was that actress broad that Fatty Arbuckle crushed when he was banging her?"

"Virginia Rappe, Mickey, but that was never proved. There was some question about her death."

"Yeah, Virginia Rappe, that was her name. Before the Arbuckle thing, she got knocked up by some producer she was screwing and gave the kid away. Some foster home. As that kid grew up, you know, as she started to learn a little about herself, she maybe coulda come to hate Hollywood and all that crap her mom went through. An obsession, you know. Hey, I keep sayin' she but it could be a guy. Don't know if her baby was a girl or a boy. That kid would be what, today, in their thirties? Could hate Mack Sennett and everybody who was involved in that shit."

That was an angle worth thinking about. I finished my salmon and took another hit on my Early Times.

"That kid could be your shooter, Jakester."

"That's quite a notion, pardner. Maybe so. It'd be darn hard to find him or her after all this time. The trail would be ice cold. But I'll give it some thought. A thirty-something woman? Yeah, hell of a thought there. Thanks, man."

We finished our dinners and split the bill. As we parted, I told Mickey Cohen to keep his chin up, and he said, "See you in church, kid."

When I got into my car and fired up the engine, I thought, How in the hell could I find a person Virginia Rappe sent off to foster care more than thirty years ago?

When I got home, I told Valerie about Cohen's idea and she agreed it was a good one. "Tomorrow," I said,

"I'll have Bambi check all the foster homes in the area and see if any of them were operating in 1917 or '18. Then I'll call on any that had, and see what I can find out."

"It won't be easy, Jake. Foster homes have strict privacy rules. They don't give out information willy-nilly on their wards." I knew she was right.

While I was out, Valerie had whipped up a chicken casserole, which we had for dinner. I complimented her on how good it was. We had a bottle of chardonnay to go along with it.

After I did the dishes—after all, she'd done the cooking—we listened to *The Shadow* on the radio. Lamont Cranston made himself invisible a couple of times while seeing justice done and the bad guy apprehended.

THIRTEEN

At the office in the morning, Bambi brought me coffee. She usually wore a skirt and blouse but today she had on a snug-fitting sweater, tight blue jeans and sparkly-looking sandals. I had to admit she had some flair. I thanked her for the coffee.

"By the way, Mr. Weaver, I'm graduating in June, you know. I hope you'll come to the ceremony."

"If I'm invited," I said.

"Oh, I'll see that you're invited. Now, what's up for today?" she asked. "I've got all morning. No classes till this afternoon."

I told her about contacting local foster homes and seeing which, if any, had been around back in the late teens. She gave me a quizzical look.

"Virginia Rappe," I explained, "the victim in that Fatty Arbuckle scandal back then, gave up an illegitimate child she had. Put the kid in a foster home. I'd like to track down that person if possible. It's a real long shot."

"And this might connect to the Mack Sennett shooting? This is fascinating, Mr. Weaver. Guess I'll start by looking up foster homes in the yellow pages."

"Atta girl," I said, and off she scampered, her honey-blond ponytail swinging behind her. Man, if I was single and twenty years younger, I thought for a moment, but then told myself: Knock off that crap, you're not twenty years younger and you have a fabulous wife.

I checked in with our network news office in New York to see if there was anything pressing they wanted me to do today. The producer suggested I look into why Maureen Connolly—"Little Mo"—wasn't going to defend her title at the Australian Open. The great young tennis star from San Diego had become a media darling after winning tennis's Grand Slam two years in a row.

I called Nelson Fisher, a sportswriter acquaintance on the *San Diego Union* to get Maureen's phone number.

Fisher had been a big supporter and father figure to the young tennis phenom. He gave me the number and we chatted a while about mutual acquaintances like columnists Jim Murray and Jack Murphy. Then I called Miss Connolly's number but got no answer after seven or eight rings.

I checked in with Bambi to see how she was doing. She'd reached four or five foster homes so far but none of them had been around before 1920. "I'll keep after it," she promised, and returned to her list.

I figured Maureen Connolly was out on a tennis court or somewhere and I'd try her again later, so I took two of the names from Bambi's list and tried them myself. The woman who answered at the first place said they opened their doors in 1941. A man at the second said he had no idea, he'd only been working there a few weeks, and that I'd have to ask the child welfare supervisor, who wasn't in that day.

"Bingo," Bambi called from the other room. "I got one, Mr. Weaver. 'Angels' Hands.' It's in Downey. They started in 1910."

I got the address from her, gave her arm a thank-you touch, and headed for the door.

Twenty-five minutes later in Downey I pulled up in front of Angels' Hands, an old Victorian wood-and-brick building of three floors, bulging with gables and turrets. The place looked as if it came from Orson Welles's *The Magnificent Ambersons.*

The supervisor turned out to a weathered, bespectacled man probably in his late sixties who was as unyielding as Stonewall Jackson. My being a CBS newsman didn't impress him at all.

"Our records from that period are sketchy at best," he told me, "and in any event I couldn't possibly let you look at them. They're absolutely confidential. I'd be breaking the law if I let you see them."

I insisted that this was a special situation which could possibly lead to solving a murder attempt. I even lied that I could get a court order. The crotchety old guy laughed at that and dared me to try.

As I drove away in defeat, I realized this would be a hugely difficult effort. Hell, I didn't even know the name I'd be looking for. It probably wouldn't be Rappe, more likely Doe, as in Jane or John Doe. Maybe at the next one, if there would even *be* a next one, I could try bribery.

When I got back to Columbia Square it was noon and Bambi had gone off to class at USC, but she'd left me a progress report. She'd found two more foster homes that had been operating back in the teens, one in El Monte and the other in Inglewood. She said she would do the Inglewood one and I could take El Monte.

I was surprised, hadn't planned on asking her to visit one of these places on her own. I had to admit it showed initiative. I wondered how she would do.

I had a quick lunch in our KNX cafeteria, then headed east on Valley Boulevard to El Monte and the home called Presbyterian Pathways.

This place turned out to be two long wooden buildings resembling army barracks with a fenced playground between them. Several kids were out there using the play equipment.

I hiked up a cracked concrete walkway to the building on the left, which had an OFFICE sign over its door. Soon I was in with the supervisor, a thin, youngish man in a white shirt and necktie, his suit coat draped over the back of his chair.

I introduced myself, sat in the visitor chair he indicated, and tossed my fedora on a side table. A couple of diplomas and a painting of Christ hung on the barnwood wall behind him. After I introduced myself, he said he was Charlie Barnes, ordained pastor and child welfare counselor. We shook hands and I stated my business.

"Why on earth would you want to see what wards we had here back in those years?" he asked.

I went through it all, saying that Virginia Rappe's child might possibly be a connection to last week's shooting of Mack Sennett. Dust motes eddied in the sunlight seeping in from partly-open Venetian blinds.

"Nasty business, that shooting of Mr. Sennett," Barnes said. "It's a blessing that he wasn't killed. But as to Virginia Rappe's child, do you have reason to believe he or she was here in our place?"

"None whatever, Reverend," I admitted. "All we know is that the child was placed in foster care somewhere, probably in the L.A. area because Miss Rappe was in the movies. It's a needle in a haystack kind of thing."

"Do you know the child's name?" he asked.

"No, and not even the gender, only the mother's name."

"Then it certainly is a needle in a haystack, Mr. Weaver. If I were you, I'd try the Los Angeles County Social Services Center. If anyone has records of foster children from that time period, they would. They get informed about every child taken in at any foster home in the county. Their records for recent years are impeccable and reliable. But I wouldn't know about that far back."

I should have known that some County agency would have purview over foster homes. I said, "Good suggestion, Reverend, we'll do that. But about your records here . . . "

"Couldn't possibly let you see them," he interrupted. "Stringent privacy rules, you see. I'm sorry."

"Suppose I arranged a contribution to this home or to the Presbyterian Church," I tried.

With a knowing smile, Charlie Barnes said, "That would be gratefully accepted, of course, but it would not open our pages to your eyes."

"That was what I figured, Reverend."

"Are you a church-goer, Mr. Weaver?" he asked.

"I'm not a member anywhere, but my wife and I go to Hollywood Presbyterian once in a while."

"That's a wonderful church. Dr. Evans is a splendid pastor. You should go more often."

"You're probably right. Well, thank you for your time, Reverend." I got up and retrieved my hat. He said he was sorry he couldn't have helped as I left.

Driving away, I thought, Well, bribery didn't work.

FOURTEEN

Back at the office, I managed to reach Maureen Connolly when I tried again. She said she was a little worn down after winning all the big tournaments the last two years and wanted to skip the Australian Open because it was such a long and tiring trek. She would still play in the other big ones, the French and U.S. Opens, and Wimbledon.

Which of those was her favorite, I asked, and without hesitation she answered Wimbledon. She wanted to know how I got her number and I said from sportswriter Nelson Fisher. "He's a sweet man, like an uncle to me," she replied.

Her wanting to dodge the long trip to Melbourne wasn't a big story, but I typed it up on the teleprinter and sent it off to New York.

In the morning, Bambi bounced into the office even more energetically than usual. "I think I struck gold at the foster home in Inglewood," she gushed, practically dancing from foot to foot.

"Sounds great," I said, "but cool your jets there, girl. Sit down and tell me about it."

She popped into the chair at my desk and said, "The place in Inglewood is called 'Every Child.' It opened in 1910. Well, in 1918, Virginia Rappe dropped off a baby girl there. They named her Betty Jones and raised her till her teen years. At age 16 she got a job at Kresge's five and dime. At 18 she left the home, got an apartment or something, and they lost track of her. She was supposed to keep in touch and let them know how she was doing but she never did. So the last they heard about her was in 1936."

"That's fine detective work, Sugar." Without thinking about it, I leaned in and gave her a little kiss on the cheek. She gave me an I-deserved-that grin. "How did you ever get all that?" I asked.

"The supervisor was out so I talked to his assistant, a skinny young man not much older than me. He was pretty shy. I flirted outrageously and told him how important this could be. I think he got the impression that he could ask me out. Silly boy. As if."

Bambi Scott will go far, I told myself.

"Well done. Thanks to you, we know that a Betty Jones was working at a Kresge's store in 1936. A Kresge's here in L.A., I assume?"

"Oh, gee, I didn't ask that, Mr. Weaver, but I think so."

"That's all right. I would think so, too. That was eighteen years ago. It will be a darn cold trail but at least we've got something to work with."

"I guess the next step," she asked, "would be for me to check with Kresge's L.A. headquarters and see what I can find out?"

"Atta girl. Yes, please do that. I appreciate your initiative and enthusiasm, Bambi."

Now it was her turn to kiss my cheek, which she did, not as one would do with an old friend but with some energy in it, then bounded off to her desk in the other room.

I thought about that remarkable young woman for a moment—I had to admit, that kiss had felt good—but then, back to business. Logical thought surfaced. This was still a needle in a very huge haystack. No young woman would remain at a low-paying clerk's job in a five and dime forever. If Bambi finds anything at Kresge's it will be that a Miss Betty Jones worked there a while and then left. And went where? Anyone's guess.

An hour later, Detective Wannamaker showed up unexpectedly. "Hey, Weaver," he said, "got a minute?"

"Sure," I said and waved the cop to the visitor's chair. He took off his hat and placed in on his knee.

"How's your daughter doing?" Wanamaker, who'd investigated Ilse's stabbing by a Nazi fugitive a few years ago, often asked about her. He'd been impressed by her strength and courage.

"She's doing fine. She's a reporter on the Pasadena paper."

"Good to hear. Give her my regards. Now, on the Sennett thing, I'm not getting anywhere," he confessed. "Are you? I know you and I know you're trying to figure out who shot Sennett, don't try to tell me you're not."

"Well yeah, pardner, I've been thinking on it a bit. For starters, I'm sure Hal Roach had nothing to do with it. Why would he, after all these years? It's got to be somebody else, somebody from way back in the twenties who still holds a grudge, thinks Sennett wronged them somehow." I was going to keep Betty Jones close to my vest. She was my lead, not his.

"And you're still convinced the shooter was a

woman?"

"Not convinced, Owen, but fairly sure. That was my impression. Didn't get a good look, as I've told you before. Man, I was ducking!"

"Now don't laugh at this, Jake, but I'd like you to see a hypnotist we sometimes use. If you're willing."

"A hypnotist?"

"Right, a woman psychologist, has a doctorate from Cal. Under hypnosis, she's often helped people recall things they otherwise couldn't. Pull things out of their subconscious. We've seen it work. It's helped us on a few cases. What do you say? Will you see her?"

I'd never been hypnotized before. Never even thought about it. It would be an interesting experience, something different. And if it could help?

After a moment, I said, "Sure. Why not?"

FIFTEEN

That afternoon I found myself in the Beverly Hills office of a Dr. Charlotte Edmonds. She looked to be in her late forties with short, graying hair, an oval face and a pleasant smile. She wore a simple black dress and no jewelry.

There was no desk in the room, just easy chairs and an upholstered sofa circling a low coffee table. An Impressionist-looking painting and a couple of diplomas hung on walls painted a robin's-egg blue.

"It's so nice to meet you, Mr. Weaver," she said, waving me to one of the chairs, seating herself in one directly opposite so that we were facing each other. "Would you care for some water or fruit juice?"

I said no thanks I was fine and she continued, "I'm an

accredited hypnotherapist and I've often worked with the police to help them come up with some information they otherwise hadn't been able to obtain. Have you ever been hypnotized or know much about it?"

"No, doctor, never hypnotized."

"It's a technique that seeks to create a changed state of awareness and uncover some genetic memory. We find that hypnosis-induced relaxation can often lead to improved focus and concentration." She was speaking in a gentle, calm tone of voice. "Are you with me so far?"

"Yes, I understand."

"I've been told that you were beside Mr. Sennett last week when unfortunately he was shot."

I agreed that was right and she said, "I've also been told that you didn't get a good look at the person who did the shooting but that your impression is that it was a woman, is that correct?"

"That's right."

Now she looked more directly into my eyes, not in a threatening way but more in the manner of a gentle grandmother.

"Are you ready?" she asked. I nodded that I was.

"Splendid. Now take a deep breath, Mr. Weaver, then release it slowly as if blowing out a candle. That's it. Now I want you to relax. Simply relax. Close your eyes, please." I closed them.

"Feel yourself beginning to relax." Her voice very soothing now. "Relax, Mr. Weaver, relax. You're beginning to feel tension drift from your head down through your shoulders and into your arms." Her voice even softer. "Your eyelids are getting heavy. Your workaday concerns are drifting, drifting down, seeping through your shoulders and into your arms." Her voice almost hushed. "Drifting down, drifting down. Your tension is draining through your arms and into the ends of your fingers." Just whispering now. "You're relaxing more and more. The tension is in your hands and fingers, drifting out of your body. Drifting out, out of your body."

I did feel a tingling in my fingers. I was in a kind of mellow haze.

"You're very relaxed now, very relaxed. Almost asleep."

She said nothing for a while, maybe a minute or two. My fingers still tingled.

Then, softly: "Look back now to that day last week. You're walking beside Mr. Sennett. Two people are approaching. You see them again now. You see them. One of them draws a gun. You see that person's face, just for a moment, but you see it. You can see it. Look at that face again now. You see it, Mr. Weaver. You see it."

I could. At first it was a murky, gauzy image but it

slowly came into focus. There it was, the face. It wasn't there long, but for a moment I could make it out. Long black hair, falling below the ears. Blue eyes. Subtle nose, slender nostrils. No powder or lipstick. Dimpled chin jutting a little, a good feminine chin. For a flicker of a second I thought I recognized the face, but that was gone just as fast. There was something off about that chin, though. Now I could make out a little strip of darkness as if the chin was almost but not quite in need of a shave.

A shave? This face wasn't feminine, it was *masculine*! All but the hair. That was a woman's hair. But this face was a man's. With some 5 o'clock shadow.

"What do you see, Mr. Weaver?" she asked gently. "What do you see?"

"The face of a man . . . but with long woman's hair."

"Describe the face, Mr. Weaver."

I did as she asked. The eyes, the nose, the chin, the lack of makeup.

"Thank you, Mr. Weaver. Now just relax some more, and open your eyes when you feel ready."

I slowly opened them—and blinked. I still felt very relaxed, as if I'd just woken from a deep sleep.

"You saw a man who wore a woman's wig, is that right?"

"Yes, Dr. Edmonds, I think I did."

"Thank you, Mr. Weaver. You did very well. How do you feel?"

"I feel, well, refreshed, doctor. Yeah, refreshed. Rested up."

"Perhaps now you'd like something to drink."

"I would, yes. Some water would be fine."

As I drank from a cup of water, she said she'd make a report to Detective Wannamaker. And then, "Something else is on your mind, isn't it, Mr. Weaver? You're uneasy about something. I sense it."

So I told her about the nightmares I've had since being shot at it in Germany, and my panic attack Saturday at the Pike when it felt like those crazy mirrors were firing at me.

"Hypnosis can sometimes help with that as well, Mr. Weaver. I've assisted a few people who've had trouble sleeping. Would you consider that?"

I said maybe so, I'd think about it, and might call her one of these days to make an appointment.

As I drove away, still feeling remarkably refreshed, I thought, Wow, the person who fired at Sennett wasn't a woman at all, but a man disguised as one.

That night Valerie was eager to hear all about the hypnosis experiment, asking me question after question over dinner. I told her that I found the episode intriguing, rather relaxing, something like a good nap, but most importantly it enabled me to envision a face I hadn't perceived on the day of the shooting.

"I know another way to get relaxed, Sailor," she cooed, and gave me The Look.

That was enough invitation for me. I kissed her on the lips, then reached over and gently bit her earlobe. Next I blew lightly into that ear, just a tiny breath. I felt her body shudder. I kissed her on the neck, her lovely neck, and we were off and running. We were in the bedroom with our clothes off in a matter of seconds.

SIXTEEN

In the a.m., we shared a morning-after breakfast full of eye contact and touching that said, Wow, that was something. But damn, we both had jobs we needed to get to.

When I arrived at nine at Columbia Square, Bambi greeted me with both coffee and a disheartened look.

"Thanks for the java," I said. "Why the long face?"

"At Kresge's L.A. headquarters they had no idea what became of Betty Jones. Their employee records don't go back as far as '36. So I called their world headquarters in Detroit, long distance. I hope that was okay."

"Course it was. We can afford it."

"Same thing there. They said, 'Sorry, CBS, but we

can't help you. We don't keep track of where our people go after they leave our employ.' "

I took a drink from my coffee mug and said, "You can wipe that sad look off your face, Bambi. That was a nice effort, good legwork, but it wasn't Betty Jones who shot Mack Sennett, or any other woman."

"Really? No other woman?" Wide-eyed now. "What have you found out, Mr. Weaver?"

I told her about the hypnosis session and the face it conjured up, the face of a man wearing a woman's wig.

"Jeepers," Bambi uttered. "What an experience for you. But I still wonder whatever happened to Betty Jones, if she ever knew anything about her mother, if she ever got married and had kids."

Those were good reporter's instincts.

"You're a great journalist, Mr. Weaver," she went on, "and I'm always learning from you. Maybe we could solve the Black Dahlia murder case."

"We?" I said, flabbergasted. "Solve the Black Dahlia?" She was referring to the gruesome mutilation and murder of 22-year-old Elizabeth Short back in '47. The star-struck young woman had been bisected at the midsection and dumped nude in a vacant lot. The L.A. cops and FBI never solved the case. It made sensational headlines for weeks.

"Sure," Bambi gushed. "With your reporting skills

and my energy and enthusiasm, we'd make a great team. We could solve it."

Before I could raise one of my several objections, the phone rang and she bounded off to answer it.

"It's Detective Sergeant Wannamaker," she called.

I picked up the receiver and Wannamaker thanked me for seeing Dr. Edmonds. "I appreciate you going there, Weaver. I kind of had a hunch all along we might be looking for a man rather than a woman. Now we're pretty sure. We're keeping that quiet, though, not telling the press. Better for our investigation, let the guilty party think we're on the wrong track. Keep that mum, Weaver, okay?"

He'd just told the press but I said sure, then asked, thinking the shooter might have tossed it while scampering away, "Did anybody pick up a black wig anywhere near the shooting scene?"

"That woulda been nice, but nope, nobody found a wig."

"By the way, you weren't on the Black Dahlia case back in the day, were you?" I said.

"Nope, I didn't draw that one. Why do you ask?"

"No reason. Somebody happened to mention it today, is all."

"Well, thanks again, and I'll be in touch," he said and rang off.

I thought again about Bambi's off-the-wall idea that the grizzled old newsman and the bouncy young journalism student could solve the Black Dahlia.

It had been a shocking and sensational murder case. I was on the *Herald-Express* at the time and I remembered it well. One suspect was George Hodel, a doctor well known for his womanizing, and he had the medical skills to bisect a human body. Another was L.A. nightclub owner Mark Hansen, whose name had showed up underlined in the victim's address book.

Yet another theory was that Norman Chandler, publisher of the *Times*, had got Miss Short pregnant and arranged for mobster Bugsy Siegel to get rid of this awkward problem for him. I knew Chandler had an appetite for young women, that he was tight with Siegel, and that Bugsy was capable of doing the deed. The cops followed this and other leads but never got anywhere. I'd long suspected Chandler had the influence to get the cops to look the other way.

The case still remained open.

I called Hal Roach and arranged to come by his studio this afternoon and collect the Laurel and Hardy footage he was lending me for the documentary. Next I called my daughter Ilse at the *Star-News* and asked if she could come over for dinner tonight. She had long-laid dinner plans with an old girlfriend, but suggested late afternoon coffee in Pasadena. She got off work at 3.

"Bambi," I called out, "what's your class load today? I was wondering if you could you go by the Hal Roach Studio in Culver City and pick up some film he has for me."

"I have a class at 1, Mr. Weaver, but I'm free after that. Sure, I'll go out there for you. I've never seen that studio."

At 3:15 I met up with Ilse at a place called Rod's Diner. Not wanting to spoil our appetites for dinner, we each had coffee and a doughnut, mine chocolate, hers glazed.

"So good to see you, *Vati*," she said as we hugged before settling into seats at a booth. I was pleased that she still liked to call me by the German word for daddy. Ilse had been born in Germany, daughter of a woman with whom I'd had a brief affair in 1930, years before I met Valerie. I'd been there for the memorial service for my late Aunt Marta. Not wanting me to feel trapped, Ilse's mother, Winifrid, didn't tell me she'd become pregnant. She ran afoul of the Nazis, got hauled off to a concentration camp, and murdered. Little Ilse was sent off to an orphanage.

I didn't learn of Ilse's existence till 1942 when she was 12. I had sneaked into Nazi Germany on a covert mission for President Roosevelt and MI6. Ilse and I managed to flee Germany through Sweden and she did the rest of her growing up here in L.A. with Valerie and me.

She asked how I was doing in trying to figure out who shot Mack Sennett and I told her about our wild goose chase after Virginia Rappe's daughter before learning through hypnosis that the assailant likely was a man, not a woman.

Ilse wanted to know all about the hypnosis, so I described it, emphasizing how relaxing and refreshing it felt.

Then she said, "Did you see that interview the *Daily News* did with Everett Hensley, where he said he should have gotten your job at CBS? Said he was better qualified and that the fix was in."

"Yeah, he's just a sore loser. I wouldn't waste a second worrying about what Hensley says."

I took a bite of my doughnut, then cut to the chase. "Ilse, Valerie and I are wondering why you've been down to visit Kenny and Claudia so much lately. It seems a little excessive."

"Well, I like them, *Vati*, enjoy their company."

"Your stepmom thinks maybe you're enjoying Kenny's company a little too much. Is she off-base on that?"

"Kenny's a little unhappy, *Vater*." Oh oh, when Ilse switched from daddy to father, I knew she was getting serious. "He feels that Claudia is kind of looking down on him, she being a doctor and all, while he's just a teacher. But that makes no sense. He coauthored a great book with you, while Claudia's never written a book or anything like that."

"So you've been giving him a shoulder to lean on, someone to tell his troubles to?" I asked.

Ilse bit at her lower lip. "Not exactly but, well, sort of." Said quietly.

"I have two things to say to that, girl. One, Claudia's probably feeling kind of insecure right now, trying to get her practice up and running, trying to develop a patient base and her insecurity might be limiting her feel-good time with Kenny. And two, they're married, it's their situation to work out, not yours or mine or any third party's."

"I know that's right, *Vati*, but it's not what you think at all."

"Mostly you talk with Kenny, is that right? Not so much with Claudia?"

"Well, yeah. He has an hour or so after school before Claudia's office hours are over, so we've gotten together to talk—but only twice. There's a coffee shop not far from the school."

I reached out and laid a hand on top of my daughter's. For one of the first times I noticed how much of her mother I saw in her face. The same nose, the same dimple in the cheeks when she smiled. It gave me an achy feeling. She'd inherited my reddish hair but more of Winni's face. "Are you and Kenny starting to have feelings for each other," I asked, "a little more than just friendship?" I could see on her face that she would have trouble answering that.

"Oh, Ilse," I said, "back off on that. Let them work through it on their own. They fell in love during the war when she nursed him for his wounds at Guadalcanal. It was a fraught time for them and they needed each other. What they have is deep and strong, and it doesn't need any emotional distractions from a well-meaning and lovely woman like you. That can only do harm. Am I making sense to you?"

"Of course you are. But there's something else that I can't tell you about. Someday I will be able to, but not now." She paused for a lingering moment, then finally said, "So please don't worry, *Vati*, because there's nothing to worry about."

Nothing to worry about?

I didn't want our visit to end on that note, so I asked what stories she was working on for the *Star-News*, how her apartment was, and so on. She said she'd like

Valerie and me to come over for dinner one of these nights and I said we'd sure do that.

After a hug and goodbye kiss on the cheek, I left wondering what was this something else that my strong-minded daughter couldn't tell me.

That night at home I told Valerie all about the conversation with Ilse. My wife said, "Ilse's a clever girl. She's got something up her sleeve. I think it might be a good idea if I went to see Claudia, just me, and you visited Kenny."

We were sitting in the living room enjoying some after-dinner brandy. I agreed that would be a good idea, then asked, "What's going on at the plant, Sweets?"

"We're going to have a big dinner in a couple of weeks honoring our founder, Allan Lockheed. He's 65 now and no longer one of the owners, but still revered as an aviation pioneer. He developed the Lockheed Vega, one of the most successful planes of the '30s. It was the plane of choice for Amelia Earhart and Wiley Post.

"Old Mr. Lockheed comes around as a consultant from time to time, but I've never met him. This shindig will be at the Biltmore. You'll have to wear your tux, if it still fits."

I stuck out my tongue and said, "It still fits!"

SEVENTEEN

Bambi came in the next morning with the can of Laurel and Hardy film I was borrowing from Hal Roach.

As she set it on my desk she enthused, "What a great time I had out there. Mr. Roach showed me around his two sound stages, editing room and so on. And he raved about a young writer who's done some work for him. His name is Rod Serling. He says Mr. Serling is highly imaginative and has written some nice things. He's done a teleplay called *Requiem for a Heavyweight,* about a once-great but now washed-up prizefighter, and about corruption in boxing. He thinks it's got a good chance to be on "Playhouse 90." He also said Serling has an idea for a TV show that would place ordinary people in paranormal situations, time warps and stuff like that. Roach says he'll try to help him shop that idea around."

"Damned interesting, Bambi. This Serling sounds like someone I'd like to meet and maybe do a story on. And thanks for picking up this film."

"No problem, Mr. Weaver. What's on for today?"

"We're pretty sure now that the person who shot Mack Sennett was a man. So we don't worry anymore about whatever happened to Betty Jones after she left Kresge's. We know that Sennett's studio didn't survive the Depression. He declared bankruptcy in 1934 after a deal he had with Paramount went south. Maybe somebody who got hurt by that, one of his debtors . . ."

"Yeah," Bambi interrupted, "sure, somebody thirsting for revenge."

"Thirsting for revenge?" I said with a chuckle. "That's pretty melodramatic, Bambi, but yeah, that's what I was thinking. And another thing, there was a nasty road accident in Mesa, Arizona around then, 1934 I think. Sennett was injured and an actor friend, Charles Mack, was killed. Maybe our shooter was some friend or relative of Charles Mack's."

"Who was responsible for the accident, Mr. Weaver? Was Mr. Sennett driving?"

"Calling me Mr. Weaver all the time makes me feel

old, Bambi. We've worked together for weeks now. You think maybe you could call me Jake?" Her grin said yes, she could. "As to who was responsible, I don't know the details. I'll ask Sennett next time I see him, maybe today. Yeah, today. Might as well do a story on how he's doing."

"Are you still coming to my graduation, Jake?" she asked.

"Sure. My wife and I will be glad to."

"Your wife? Oh yeah, I guess you'd want her to come, too."

"Of course, Bambi. Now, will you call Hal Roach and get contact information for this Rod Serling fellow?"

"Sure thing, Mr. Weaver. Oops, I mean Jake. Don't forget about the Black Dahlia. We could do it!" Bambi touched my hand and winked before swinging off, excitement in her steps. She liked getting assignments, and she'd obviously enjoyed meeting Roach. But I'd have to dissuade her from this Black Dahlia notion. And also do something about this darn flirting.

On my way to Mount Sinai Hospital, I stopped at a liquor store and bought a little something for Sennett. When I arrived outside his room twenty-five minutes later, a different cop was sitting there in a chair, looking bored, sucking on a toothpick. He looked over my CBS credential and waved me in without frisking me.

It wouldn't be too hard for an assassin to get past that guy, I thought.

I found Mack looking considerably improved since my last visit. He was still connected to various wires and tubes but he was sitting up with more color in his cheeks and a newspaper in his hands. I was disappointed to see it was the *Times* and not the *Herald-Express*, even though I didn't work there anymore. Loyalty runs deep. On his bedside stand was a glass of water with a bent straw in it to make drinking easier.

I dropped into the chair beside his bed and set down at my feet what I'd brought in a brown paper sack. We exchanged pleasantries, me asking how he was feeling and him saying good to see me. Then I asked, "Mack, about that traffic fatality in Arizona back in the '30s. What do you remember about that?"

"There was a blackface comedy team," he began, "Charlie Mack and George Moran. They were kind of a poor man's Amos 'n' Andy. They billed themselves as the Black Crows on the vaudeville circuit. In those days, blackface was considered good comedy, although I never cared for it. I think it disrespects and degrades Negroes. I wish the Amos 'n' Andy show would get canceled.

"Anyway, I'd been in New York directing a film of theirs. They'd also just wrapped a vaudeville gig in Brooklyn and their next job was on the coast. 'Why don't you ride out with us?' Charlie asked. I was a little nervous about flying, those crates were pretty flimsy in those days, so I said okay.

"And off we went, Charlie and Moran in that big Lincoln of theirs, plus me and Charlie's wife Myrtle and their daughter, Mary Jane. Charlie and Myrtle were in front, I was in the back seat with Moran and Mary Jane."

"You were where, in the middle?" I asked.

"No, I was on the right side of the back, Mary Jane in the middle, and Moran on the left. Charlie was driving pretty fast. Myrtle said a couple of times that he oughta take it easy. Well, just before Phoenix a tire blew, and the car swerved outta control. Flipped three or four times and ended upside down in a sandy wash beside the road."

Mack stopped and took a sip of water before going on. "Then came the worst moments of my life. No, make that the second worst. The worst was the other day when you saw me get shot. Anyway, we were all banged up and hurt, the women moaning and bawling. Poor Myrtle began wailing her head off when she saw that Charlie wasn't breathing. He looked like his chest got crushed by the steering wheel. The rest of us were pretty bad hurt and bloody, too.

"First, a deputy sheriff car showed up and a little later an ambulance. Turns out I had a concussion and a broken left wrist, Moran a broken arm and some lacerations; the women fared the best, at least physically. What a sad, sad day. Weeks later, Moran quipped in the papers that this was the Black Crows' last flight. I didn't find that funny."

"Is George Moran still alive?" I asked, wondering if he could have been the shooter in the mistaken belief that Sennett had been responsible for his partner's death.

"Nope, he passed away a few years ago, Jake. As to the women, Myrtle and Mary Jane, I have no idea."

So much for George Moran as a suspect, I thought.

I turned to the documentary I was working on. "Do you have some Keystone Kops footage I could borrow?"

"Smooth segue, Weaver," he said. It was good to see a grin on his big face. "Sad to say, a lot of that film's been lost because of poor storage. In the early days we didn't realize cellulose nitrate film had to be kept refrigerated. We still have some of those cop films, though, but what I'd really like to lend you is my first full-length comedy, *Tillie's Punctured Romance*. This featured Chaplin, Marie Dressler and my lovely Mabel." I knew he meant

Mabel Normand. "Instead of starring the Keystone Kops, I used them as background, pretty darn effective background. This was in 1914 if I remember right. We still have three or four prints, all in good shape."

"That'd be swell, Mack. I'd like to use some excerpts from that, especially with Chaplin in it. I promise we'll take good care of the print. How long are they gonna keep you in here?"

"Another great segue, Weaver. Well, they say starting tomorrow they'll have me get up and walk a few steps. Somebody'll be holding my arm. We'll see how that goes and how my balance is before making any decisions."

"Have you had any nightmares about the shooting?" I asked.

"They've had me so drugged up if I've had any dreams I don't remember them. Why do you ask?"

I'd asked because of my own nightmares about being shot at, but I decided not to go there.

"No reason, pardner, just curious." I opened the paper bag I'd brought and pulled out a bottle of Bushmills Irish whisky. I knew he was proud of his Canadian-Irish heritage. "They probably won't let you have any of this in here," I said, "but put it with your things and enjoy it at home when you get out of here."

Mack thanked me profusely and said he'd tuck it

under the spare pillow for now. I took my leave, shaking his hand and saying, "I'm pulling for you, Mack. You're going to be fine."

As I drove away, I wondered why he directed a Moran and Mack film in '32 when he didn't care for blackface. But the Depression was on, his business was struggling, and so he probably needed the money.

I was no closer to finding out who shot Mack Sennett but at least was making progress on the documentary.

EIGHTEEN

Valerie and I made plans to go to San Diego on Friday afternoon to visit Kenny and Claudia Nielsen. We hoped to see them both separately and together. We'd spend the night and return home on Saturday. Valerie had some vacation time coming and could easily take a day off.

We decided that I would go and meet with Kenny after his school hours and Valerie would go to Claudia's office for a physical checkup from the newly minted doctor and some woman-to-woman conversation. Afterward, the four of us would hook up for dinner.

Claudia's practice was in a two-story red brick

building that doubled as their home in the eastern San Diego neighborhood of Rolando Park. Her medical office occupied the ground floor, while she and Kenny made their residence upstairs. Kenny taught history and coached basketball at a new high school a mile or two east in the town of La Mesa.

It was a bright spring day as I drove the Chevy down to San Diego. The new freeway under construction extended into part of Orange County before giving way to old U.S. 101.

Valerie suddenly said, "Ann Sothern and Joan Blondell." It was a little game we played, naming actors who were so similar they were virtually interchangeable.

"Yeah, I see that," I said. "Pretty good." After a moment's thought, I said, "Sterling Hayden and Robert Ryan."

As we passed Camp Pendleton, Valerie exclaimed, "Oh look, the ocean is so pretty out there. It's sparkling in the afternoon sun like diamonds."

I gassed up the buggy at a Flying A station in Carlsbad where a kid in a forest green jumpsuit cleaned the windshield and checked the oil.

On the road again, Valerie asked if I'd had any more death threats from thugs supporting Joe McCarthy. "No. Well, maybe. The other day I took a call and no one spoke. I heard somebody breathing heavily, but that was all. After saying hello two or three times I hung up. That shook me a little."

Later, when we reached the high school, I hopped out to go and meet Kenny. "I'll see what I can find out," Valerie said as she slipped behind the wheel to drive to Claudia's office.

I found Kenny waiting for me in his classroom in Building Two as we'd arranged. He said it was great to see his coauthor and we exchanged handshakes and shoulder clasps. He was using a wooden cane, having had a leg badly injured in Korea. He showed me around his classroom, hobbling a little. He'd decorated the walls with maps and historical drawings: Napoleon with his right hand sticking inside his tunic, Washington crossing the Delaware, and a photo of Teddy Roosevelt pontificating from his bully pulpit. Instructions for a homework assignment were scrawled on the blackboard.

He suggested we go to a café called Andy's on El Cajon Boulevard, which turned out to be a homey old place. Once seated, Kenny said, "I got a royalty check the other day. It's still satisfying when they come in."

"It sure is," I agreed. "Our book has done all right. Maybe we should think about doing another."

The waitress came by and we both ordered coffee, declining cream or sugar. Then, with a guarded look on his face, Kenny said, "Yeah, another book would be great, but not for a while."

"Getting established as a teacher's taking up most of your time, hey? How's the leg coming along, pardner?"

"Getting better all the time, Jake. I do certain exercises to strengthen it. Every time they check me out at the naval hospital they tell me it's coming along well. And of course being married to a doctor's a big plus."

The coffee arrived and Kenny said, "Thanks, Kate."

"How's Claudia doing?" I asked.

"It's tough starting a new practice from scratch but she's real determined and serious about it. She's got a few patients now and they seem pleased. Claudia says they'll recommend her to others and it'll grow. There are a lot of young families in this area and the word will get around. Plus, I've been telling my fellow faculty members I know a good doctor if they need one. But there's the debt and that nags at her. The machines and other apparatus cost us a lot. I did manage to scrounge a used X-ray machine from the MCRD infirmary with the help of one of my old superior officers."

"Good for you," I said. "She'll make it. It'll be a success. Now, I hear that Ilse has been visiting you."

The guarded look pinched Kenny's face again. "Well, yeah, but just twice."

"What do you talk about?" I tried not to look concerned but probably did.

"You don't have to play the distrustful father, Jake. We're not messing around and we're not planning to elope to Brazil. We've just been exploring a mutual interest. I can't talk about it now."

"Ilse tells me the same thing, that it's nothing to worry about but she can't talk about it."

"There you are, Jake. You'll be pleased when you hear about it."

"Damn, I hate mysteries," I said, downing more of my coffee. "Well then, tell me about the teaching."

"I really like it." Kenny's face brightened. "Taking to it like a fish to water. I've always loved history and most of these students are good kids. We get along. And I like the faculty and the administration. It's really been fine."

It felt good to see and hear his enthusiasm. "How about the basketball coaching?"

"I coached the B team, which is basically the junior varsity. Season's over now, but we did okay, won more than we lost. I have the kids running cross-country now to keep their legs in shape. Most of them will make varsity next year and I'll get some new boys. The trouble is we don't have a real gym yet. It's the growing pains of a new school. We play our home games at a rival school nearby. Sometimes we get to practice in their gym too, but mostly we have to do it outdoors right here on asphalt courts. Once in a while we get to practice at a big old gym at a former military base in the valley. We're all in this together and we make do, kind of like being in the Marines."

"I'll come and see one of your games next year," I said.

"Anytime. You'd enjoy it. So, how do you like TV news compared with working on newspapers?"

"Good question," I said. "Whenever something big happens out here, naturally I report it for New York and the national feed. They give me assignments and I suggest stories on my own, but I have a lot of freedom to work on things that interest me."

"Like whatever happened to yesteryear's kings of slapstick comedy?"

"Exactly, Kenny. But I do miss the boisterous camaraderie of the newsroom, the bullshitting with the reporters and editors, the clamor of telephones and typewriters, the crude jokes, the deadlines. There was a kind of gusto in the air. Ben Hecht and Charles McCarthy got it right when they wrote *The Front Page*."

"I can picture that," Kenny said. "You experience something like that in a Marine Corps barracks. Say, have the McCarthyites given you any more grief?"

I'd had threatening phone calls and some hate mail after my piece that castigated Joe McCarthy over his claims without a shred of proof that Robert Oppenheimer was a communist.

"Except for a phone call the other day when nobody spoke, it seems to have mostly died down. It really concerns me, though, when a public official who has the ear of the media can tell lie after lie without any consequences. Tell the lie long enough and often enough and people will start to believe it. That's how Hitler got started."

Kenny nodded in agreement. He finished his coffee, took hold of his cane and said, "Well, come on, let me show you where we live."

At their home, Claudia greeted me with a hug and cheek kiss and said it was great to see me and she'd been having a fine visit with Valerie. After showing me the guest bedroom, where I tossed my small overnight bag on the chair, she said, "Come on downstairs, you have to see my office."

She proudly showed me her medical practice setup, which included a reception area and desk, where her part-time nurse hung out, doubling as receptionist. "I can't afford her fulltime yet, but that will come," she said.

Claudia led me into the other room, a larger space that served as both the examination room and her office. The walls were painted a mint green. Her framed diploma from the UCLA School of Medicine hung on one of them. "Come on, sit down there," she commanded, directing me to a chair. She picked up a sthesoscope, listened to my heart and lungs, then fastened a blood-pressure cuff on my arm and pumped it up. After a moment, she said, "That's a little high, Jake, 140 over 80. Nothing to worry about, but a tad high. Valerie had better numbers." Then, widening her arms and gesturing around, she asked, "Well, what you think of the place?"

"I'm impressed, Claudia. It looks very professional. I wish you all the luck in the world here."

"Thanks. It's a little slow getting started, but I'm, I mean we, are going to make it." Was she referring to both her practice and her marriage?

As she slid her sthesoscope into a drawer I noticed a pistol in there. "Is that a gun, Claudia?"

"Yes, one can't be too careful these days." She took my arm and said, "Let's go up and have some dinner."

Back upstairs, Kenny and Valerie were chatting over glasses of wine. Kenny put his down and quickly filled glasses for Claudia and me. "This is a California zinfandel," he said. "Hope you like it."

I raised my glass and said, "A toast! To Kenny and Claudia and success in their post-military lives." A chorus of hear hears rang out.

When we sat down to dinner I saw a nice pork tenderloin on the table, along with a tossed green salad, French bread, and a bowl of peas. Kenny lit the candles and when I remarked at how delicious the tenderloin looked, he said, "We splurged tonight in honor of you two. We often have meatloaf or takeout pizza. Got to count our pennies."

"Only till the patients start coming in," Claudia said. "The word is getting around in Rolando and La Mesa. One of my new patients is a Methodist pastor and he says he'll mention me to some of his parishioners."

"I don't know anybody at the *La Mesa Scout*," I said, "but I'll contact them, newsman to newsman, and suggest they do a feature on a new physician in the area, a woman who was a hero in the Pacific during the war. They might go for that."

"That would be swell, Jake," Claudia exclaimed. "Thanks so much."

"He's a good idea man," Kenny said as he sliced and served. "Say, Jake, are you having any luck finding out who shot Mack Sennett?"

"Not yet, but I'm finding out who *didn't* shoot him. The cops are even more stumped than I am." I mentioned the fruitless leads I'd followed regarding the tragic Fatty Arbuckle affair and the fatal Charlie Mack car crash.

Windows were open as it was a warm day and suddenly distant bugle music could be heard. "What's that?" Valerie asked.

"It's Evening Colors over at the naval radio station," Kenny said. "Remember those three big radio towers on a hill south of here? They're playing Taps and lowering the flag."

Claudia put down her fork and asked, "How's my old college roommate Ilse doing?" Did she sneak a hint of a glance at Kenny or was that my imagination? She hadn't needed to ask that. Although Ilse had spent more of her time down here with Kenny, she and Claudia had gotten together recently as well.

"She's doing great," I said. "One of the *Star-News'* best reporters."

After dinner we sat up and talked a while longer over decaf coffee before turning in. I told them about my hypnosis experience and that brought on lots of questions. Claudia asked about our own physician and how his practice was doing, Kenny wanted to know how my documentary was progressing, and Valerie told a bit about the Viking and Vanguard rockets. Kenny showed more interest in the rockets than did Claudia. She was quiet and looked a little distant.

Eventually, it was time to call it a night. "We just got the guest bedroom set up a couple of weeks ago," Kenny said. "We hope you'll like it."

"You'll be the first to use it," Claudia put in.

After saying our goodnights, we found the room pleasantly furnished with chairs, a mirrored vanity and a double bed, items which might have come from J.C. Penney or a used-furniture store. One wall held two photos, one of Kenny in Marine Corps utilities with seven or eight other guys, the other with his buddy Billy Ninetrees, a Pawnee Indian. A shadow box displayed Kenny's two Purple Hearts and another medal I couldn't name.

Valerie said, "I can't wait to hear what Kenny had to say this afternoon and I need to bring you up to date on Claudia and me." Val began unbuttoning her blouse, but in a businesslike way without giving me The Look. As I started to undress too, I said, "Kenny insists that he and Ilse visited only twice and there's nothing to worry about, but that he can tell me more at some future date. Very mysterious. And frustrating."

"And what did he have to say about him and Claudia?"

"Kenny seems pretty understanding about their

finances and her worries over making the practice a success. I think he's more positive about all of this than she is. But she's a good doctor and he's proud of her. Did she check your vitals?"

"Yes. Yours too?"

"Yeah, said my blood pressure's a little high, but not bad. So, tell me about your time alone with her this afternoon."

Val stepped out of her slip and set in on a chair. "She's scared, Kenny. This is a big step for her. You know, her alcoholic father was abusive and her overly religious mom had no time for her. She never really had friends until some nurses she worked with during the war. She's never really had a support net. Because her father was a monster, she never trusted men until she met Kenny and now I hope that's not unraveling because of her anxiety about debt. It cost a lot more than they have to get her practice up and running. She didn't say much about Kenny or their relationship at this point, and that bothers me. She ought to be very proud of him."

"I felt a disconnect in her during dinner," I said. "I also saw she had a pistol in her office."

"So did I," Valerie put in. "That worried me."

We crawled under the covers and I said, "Let's hope the patients start rolling in and they get their finances beefed up."

"Right, Jake, but I hope the old demons from her juvenile days aren't coming back. I fear they might be. Are you really going to call that local newspaper and suggest they do a story on Claudia?"

"Sure. I'll bet they'll be glad to hear about a female war hero in their neighborhood."

My gorgeous wife kissed me, but then pulled away. "I wouldn't feel right about any hanky-panky here, right next to their room."

I was usually ready for a little hanky-panky but she was right. I wondered how much hanky-panky was going on these nights in the next room.

NINETEEN

After a pleasant breakfast on Saturday morning at a pancake house on El Cajon Boulevard, we wished Kenny and Claudia good luck and said our goodbyes. "Come see us in L.A. next time," I said. "The welcome mat's always out."

As we drove off, Valerie said, "For a change of pace, let's take the inland route. We've seen a lot of 101 and the coast."

That was okay with me, so I steered us onto U.S. 395 and pointed the Chevy toward Escondido and the hill country beyond. As the miles rolled by, we agreed that our just-completed visit had been enjoyable and interesting but not very enlightening on Kenny and Claudia's relationship nor on what Kenny and my daughter Ilse might be up to.

But I did enjoy seeing Kenny's school and his classroom and I told Valerie I thought he'd be an excellent teacher.

"Claudia's a troubled woman," Valerie said. "As a child she was sexually abused by her father, a drunkard, and her mother was a religious fanatic who had little time for her. I know Kenny's good for her but she has demons."

After about an hour we passed through the little burg of Temecula. "A few miles east of here," I said, "is where old Butch Cassidy and his lady friend Juanita live, if they're still alive. Remember my finding that cagey old outlaw?"

"Of course I do, Sailor, and I admire how you kept his secret. That would have made a big story for you, finding and exposing a famous bandit who was supposed to have been killed in South America. But you respected his wishes. You impressed me with that."

"Aw, shucks, Sweets, that's the kind of guy I am."

We passed through Corona, and stopped for lunch at a roadside diner somewhere west of Pomona. Over her chicken salad sandwich, Val said, "Arlene Dahl and Rhonda Fleming."

"Yeah, coupla elegant redheads. Could be twins. Good one," I concurred, between bites of my cheeseburger. "Funny, you were just asking if the McCarthyites were giving me any more trouble, and Kenny asked me the same thing yesterday."

"Fear mongers like that are really bad for the country," she said. "They undermine the public's confidence in our democratic system."

"You couldn't be more right, Sweets."

We got home in early afternoon.

The rest of the weekend passed quickly. I spent some time reviewing my notes on the documentary and the draft script I'd started. I added some stuff about the tragic car crash in Arizona that Mack Sennett survived but had killed Charlie Mack.

I also called the *La Mesa Scout* newspaper, introduced myself to the editor and told him about the war hero nurse who was starting a medical practice there. He thanked me and said he'd call on Dr. Claudia Nielsen and interview her for a story.

I didn't know it, but on Sunday a guy in Canoga Park sat in his garage making a bomb.

On Monday it blew up my car.

TWENTY

I drove the Chevy to work on Monday and parked in my usual place behind Columbia Square. There were fourteen spots in the small lot back there, reserved for certain CBS and KNX people. One of our custodians, a young guy named Harvey, kept an eye on the place but wasn't a fulltime watchman. Our other employees had to park in pay lots or come by public transportation. A few of those, the ones with more seniority, got parking vouchers from management. The rest of the serfs were out of luck. At first I thought this was pretty heartless, but then I remembered the *Herald-Express*, which offered no parking whatsoever.

I'd arranged for Bambi, who greeted me with coffee and her classic smile, to get one of the vouchers.

Having to run to USC and back, plus errands for me, she deserved it.

"Great new song, 'Rock Around the Clock,' she told me exuberantly. "Bill Haley and the Comets. Real cool. Have you heard it yet?"

"Don't think so, Bambi."

"You will, it's all over the radio. Heard it twice already this morning." Then she threw her arms around me and said, "You're such a super guy, Jake. We could have some fun together. I mean besides solving the Black Dahlia. Why don't we go out and have dinner some night?"

"Get that idea clear out of your head, Bambi," I snarled. "I'm a happily married man and, besides, I'm way older than you. Either we keep our relationship strictly business, or you're out of here."

She gave a hurt look and murmured, "I can't help it if I'm attracted to you."

After a long silent moment, she said sheepishly, "Okay then, Jake. I hope I can still call you Jake. So what's on for today?"

I looked at this pretty young woman for a few seconds, thought seriously about canning her on the spot, but remembered the potential she had as a journalist that I'd recognized so often. Not only recognized but encouraged. I'd even thought about trying to get her a paid job here after her graduation.

After a long pause, I said, "Well, there's that big tsunami that killed a lot of people in the Aleutians, about 200 they say. Let's try and see if any of the victims had ties to some L.A. people, close relatives, that sort of thing."

Before she could answer, we heard an ear-shattering boom and the whole building seemed to shake for a moment.

"Are the Russians attacking?" Bambi said, dashing to the window that looked down on the parking lot. "Oh my god," she cried, "a car just blew up. I think it looks like yours. And the one right behind it's damaged, too."

I jumped to my feet, took a quick look—it was mine all right—and scrambled to the elevator, Bambi right behind me.

Four or five people were in the parking lot when we got there and more were arriving fast. "What happened?" someone shouted. "I called the cops," said another.

Yeah, my car had blown up, especially the front part. It looked as if most of the driver's seat had blown straight up and out through the roof. The car behind mine, a Pontiac, was nudged up tight behind mine, bumper to bumper. A dazed woman at the wheel looked shocked and hurt. Her windshield had shattered and she had some cuts on her face. I recognized her as one of the KNX executives but couldn't remember her name. I opened her driver-side door, pulled out my handkerchief and tried to blot some of her wounds. None of her cuts looked deep or life-threatening. "We'll get some help here and you'll be okay," I told her.

"What? I can't hear," she moaned.

I brushed some broken glass from her neck and shoulders and said, a little louder, "You're going to be okay. We're getting help." She must have heard. She gave a small nod and tried to smile.

"I don't know what happened," she said, as sirens wailed nearby. "I bumped that car up ahead by mistake. I must have hit the gas instead of the brake. The second I bumped that car, it just exploded. How could that happen?"

Just then a woman dashed up and shoved me away. "I'm a nurse. Let me help this lady." She began applying a soft cloth to her face, better than my hanky, and soothed her with soft words. I backed away just as a cop car wheeled in and screeched to a stop.

Two patrolmen piled out, took a quick survey of the situation, and one of them asked, "Is this woman up to talking with us?" The other got on his radio and I heard him say, "Car 14, Hollywood Division. Bomb squad, Sunset and Gower! Yeah, right away."

Before long I explained to one of the cops that the destroyed car was mine. The other took a few notes from the injured woman, who was starting to grow a little more responsive. An ambulance showed up and paramedics took over for the nurse. One of them, applying a couple of bandages, said, "I'm sure you'll be all right, ma'am, but as a precaution we'll take you to the emergency room and get you checked out. You may be suffering some shock."

About that time, I realized that Bambi was holding my hand and maybe had been for a while. I had to admit her concern was comforting. She released my hand, kissed me square on the lips—what the hell?—and scampered off, saying, "You'll want to talk with those guys. I'll start checking on possible L.A. ties to the Aleutian victims."

What was I gonna do about that hyper young lady?

During all this, our custodian Harvey showed up, looking sheepish. I wondered where the hell he'd been before that bomb went off. The car was fine when I got here, so somebody had to have come in and set up the bomb after I parked. In broad daylight.

After the slightly injured woman was taken away, I told the cop who'd been talking to her that the destroyed car was mine. He asked me a few questions and jotted down some notes. "I'm a patrolman," he said. "An incident investigator will ask you the official stuff and so will the bomb squad."

The driver-side door was hanging open, inches from being ripped off completely. I looked inside to the smoldering remains of what had been the front seat, torn metal, shattered glass and a hole in the roof. The stench of burned fabric and leather was strong.

I tried to remember if there'd been anything of value in the car. Fortunately I'd taken my briefcase, containing all my work on the documentary, up to the studio. Losing that would have been a disaster. The glove box had contained some maps and a flashlight, all replaceable. I couldn't think of anything else. I thought of all the things I'd have to do: talk to my insurance company, get a new car, and of course inform Valerie, who'd be pretty darn shaken up.

But most of all, I wondered who had tried to kill me.

A midsized black truck with LAPD Bomb Squad painted on its doors showed up a minute or two later. It consisted of two men, one carrying what looked like a black tool bag, the other a camera. I introduced myself as the owner of this wreck. The one with the bag wore denim overalls and introduced himself as Patrick Beach. "That's Greg Sowards there with the camera," he added. Greg Sowards wore khakis similar to military dungarees.

"So this thing blew with nobody in it?" Beach said. "Damn unusual—and lucky as hell for you. Where were you when it happened?"

"Upstairs," I said, pointing at the building. "I'm with CBS."

"I see. That car behind your wreck, the one with the windshield damage, is snugged up tight against yours."

"Yeah, the woman said she hit the gas instead of the brakes. She apologized."

"Well, let's see what we've got here," Beach said, and with that he put on a pair of gloves, took a flashlight and a small tool from his bag, laid down on his back, and squirmed his way under the car.

He made a few clanging noises under there and muttered some words I couldn't hear while Greg Sowards took pictures from various angles on each side of the car.

Finally, Beach scuttled back out holding what looked like the scorched remains of a shoe box and some copper wire. "About what I expected," he said, getting to his feet, "home-made bomb, fertilizer and diesel oil."

"Fertilizer?" I asked.

"Yep, ammonium nitrate, you can buy it in any garden store. It's fertilizer. Mix it with diesel oil and get yourself a detonator and you've got a bomb." He showed me a thin, silvery cylinder and said that was the detonator. "I figure he wired this to your starter but didn't do a very good job. Amateur. When the woman bumped your car this wire touched your electricals just like your starter would have, completed a circuit, and bam! Damn lucky for you she hit the gas."

That's when I saw Jerry Dunphy of KNX standing behind me with a notepad and pen in hand. "Fertilizer and diesel fuel nearly kills CBS-TV's West Coast man!"

"Aw, Jerry, no," I said. "Don't go and do a story on this."

"Got to, Jake, the other stations will find out from the police wire and we'd be scooped. It's news, buddy. Hey, I wonder if Everett Hensley knows how to make a bomb."

Hensley was the NBC guy I'd beaten out to get this job and I'd heard he was still damned upset about it. "Aw, Jer, that's sick," I said.

The bomb-squad guy, Beach, was putting the wire and the residue of the bomb in a plastic bag. "I'll file a report on this. We won't be able to tow the remains of your car to our yard for further study till the crime scene is cleared and we can get that car behind yours moved."

The registration on the steering wheel mount was

scorched but not totally destroyed, so I pulled it off, then tried to look in the trunk but it was impossible to open with that other car kissing my back bumper.

Then Detective Sergeant Wannamaker drove up.

TWENTY-ONE

The rest of the day was a blur, first Wannamaker quizzing me, then calling Valerie (terribly upset), next my insurance agent (also upset, but for a different reason) and finally thinking about renting some wheels.

I'd caused Valerie a ton of anxiety over the years. Getting nabbed by the Gestapo in Nazi Germany during the war. Trapped during the Battle of the Bulge two years later. Getting beat up by punks in D.C. with a broken foot to show for it. The list goes on. Including that panic attack I had just the other day at the Pike. Now this. Poor woman. She deserved better.

Wannamaker said that maybe hoodlum Jack

Dragna had tried to kill me, as he knew I'd run afoul of that mobster before the Bugsy Siegel murder. Dragna had tried to rub out his underworld rival Mickey Cohen with a bomb but the blast instead killed Cohen's bodyguard, who was doing the driving that day. I should say Dragna *allegedly* tried to rub out Cohen—his involvement was never proved.

I told Wannamaker, "But your bomb guy, Patrick Beach, said this job was amateurish. Dragna would have used a pro."

The detective shrugged and said that as we had a homicide attempt here, he probably would be investigating this in addition to the Mack Sennett affair. He said the car would be checked for fingerprints later at the yard. "We'll find yours and your wife's for sure and probably no one else's. The bomber likely wore gloves, but we'll check." After huddling with Patrick Beach, asking more questions of me, and much note-taking, Wannamaker left.

I cornered the custodian and said, "Where the hell've you been this morning, Harvey?"

"I'm not out here a hundred percent of the time," he said guiltily, hanging his head a little. "I got some inside duties, too."

"I don't suppose you saw any strange men hanging around here this morning?"

"No sir, Mr. Weaver, if I had I'd a done somethin' about it."

The woman who'd bumped her car into mine, causing the explosion, returned after being treated for cuts and bruises. There was a small bandage on her nose. She introduced herself as Rosie Kelleher of KNX's personnel department. Rosie apologized needlessly—hell, she'd inadvertently saved my life—and said she'd be heading to an auto-glass place as most of her front windshield was kaput.

She drove off and at last I was able to open the trunk. I saw nothing worth retrieving, except my emergency road kit—flares, first-aid stuff, et cetera—and took it out. Once my insurance agent came and tut-tutted over what was left of my 1950 Chevy Deluxe, it could be towed to the bomb squad's yard.

Bambi trotted up at that moment and said, "Jake, New York is on the line. You've gotta get back upstairs."

Miss Walker handed me the receiver and soon I was talking with Eric Sevareid, one of our senior correspondents. He brushed off my protest, saying that when someone tries to kill "one of ours" it's a story, and proceeded to interview me. After getting all the facts I could provide, he said they'd use my face shot and footage from our L.A. affiliate and produce the story for tonight's news. Oh, terrific, I thought unhappily.

Finished with the interview, Sevareid said, "Sig says rent a car and it's on us." He meant Sig Mickelson, the head of CBS News. "He says two weeks, whatever you need, the network will cover it."

After I thanked him and rang off, my old friend Marko Janicek of the *Herald-Express* showed up, notebook in hand for more of the same. *Double oh terrific.* After asking all the right questions and taking notes, Marko said, "Jake, you're the most interesting guy I've ever known. Hell of a story to write."

I'd always driven Chevys, so at the Hertz rental place I took a look at what they had in that line. The sleek Corvette caught my eye. It'd be fun to tool around in that baby for a week or two before buying a car with my insurance money. So, after showing them my driver license and press credential and signing a bunch of papers, away I went, with the top down, of course, the wind in my face. I felt pretty good for the first time in hours.

I grabbed a roast beef sandwich and Pepsi for lunch at Clifton's Cafeteria and then zipped back to Columbia Square. Man, this machine had some punch. A lot of horses under this hood. After I parked, I caught the eye of our custodian and said, "Guard these wheels with your life, Harvey, it's not mine."

When I got upstairs Bambi loped up to me and said, "Jake, I got the name of a widow here in L.A. who lost a sister in that tsunami up there. Talked to her on the phone and took a lot of notes."

I wasn't used to her calling me Jake yet but after all I had suggested it. "Good work, Bambi, type it up."

"You mean write the story myself? Me?"

"That's what I mean. You'll do a good job."

She threw her arms around me, kissed me eagerly and trotted off before I could even say, "Hey!"

Calming myself—darn that girl—I asked Miss Morgan to come in. "Please call the Hal Roach Studio," I said, "and get the number of a Mr. Rod Serling for me. He's a writer who's done some work with Roach."

Betsy nodded, gave me a coy look, swept the back of her hand across her mouth as if wiping off lipstick, and left the room.

An hour later, Miss Morgan came in and laid a small note and some papers on my desk.

"That's Mr. Serling's phone number. I found out that he's at the Roach Studios now and would like to meet you if you'd care to come out. And that's Bambi's story."

"Bambi's story? She finished it already?"

"She's fast, you know." Another sarcastic look from Betsy Morgan.

After my secretary left, I quickly read the story Bambi had written about the tsunami victims' ties to local people. It was good. I made one small edit. I grabbed my coat, hat, notebook, and Bambi's story, and went to the outer office. "Please put this on the wire to New York, Betsy. Give Bambi a byline."

Got another of those looks from Miss Morgan, which I did my best to ignore as I headed for the elevator.

I'd been toying with the idea of seeing if we could hire Bambi half-time after her graduation with our local station KNX hiring her for the other half. She'd get great experience as a reporter and splitting her salary between the network and the station might be agreeable.

When I got to my rented car, Bambi was seated comfortably in the passenger seat. "I've always wanted to ride in one of these 'Vets, Jake. Where are we going?"

TWENTY-TWO

To the Hal Roach Studio in Culver City," I said, "but first I'm dropping you at school or your sorority house, whichever works best for you."

"No no, please, don't be an old grouch. I don't have any more classes today. I'll just stand in the background and be quiet as a church mouse. By the way, was my story okay?"

It was darn good and I was in no mood to go tooling all over L.A. to drop off this young woman someplace. So off we went. "Your story was fine, Bambi. You got some nice quotes. Good job."

I wished we'd had more time when I called Valerie to tell her about the bombing. My wife was in the middle of something important with another engineer and, while upset and sympathetic, wasn't able to talk long.

As we cruised west on Hollywood Boulevard, the wind in our faces, Bambi reached over and lifted my hat off. "We don't want that blowing away, do we?" she said. "Now, about the Black Dahlia, I think the killer was that doctor, George Hodel."

"You do?"

"Sure. She jilted him after they'd had their fling and that crushed his ego. He'd probably spent a lot of money on her, nice clothes and things. He got furious. No little floozy could do that to *him*. With his medical know-how and all that razor-sharp equipment doctors have, he cut her in two, making damn sure nobody else could ever have her."

"A lot of cops thought the same thing, Bambi. You could be right, but how would we prove it?" I turned south on La Brea, the tires squealing a little. Man, this baby really purred along. I meant the car, not my passenger.

"He moved to Hawaii four years ago," Bambi said. "Doesn't that sound like what a guilty person would do? Get a lot of miles between himself and the scene of the crime?"

"Sure as hell, neither one of us is going to Hawaii to look in on Dr. Hodel," I said.

"No, Jake, but maybe we could hire a PI to follow him for a while."

"Aggie Underwood," I said, "was a crime reporter for the *Herald-Express* before they made her city editor. She was the first reporter on the scene when the body was found. She probably has some notions on this. We need to talk to Aggie. But no PI, Bambi. They don't come cheap. I've got enough nightmares as it is."

"Real nightmares? You're having nightmares?"

"Not every night, but fairly often. Somebody's always trying to kill me, to shoot me. You see, a man did fire at me in Germany a few years ago—almost took my ear off—and sometimes it still messes with my subconscious."

"Wow, Jake, my ex-boyfriend—"

"Your *ex-boyfriend*, Bambi?"

"Yeah, we broke up a few months ago. Anyway, he used to play football at USC and he got hurt pretty bad. Had nightmares for quite a while after that."

I turned south onto Venice Boulevard. Close to the Roach Studios now. "I can understand that," I said, "bad experiences coming back in the night. How come you guys broke up?"

"He was too immature for me. Too many childish

ways. Plus, he thought I was silly majoring in journalism, said I was wasting my time. He's history."

"He was damn wrong, Bambi. A free press is essential in a democracy and that requires good journalists. You'll be a good one if you stick with it." We were a couple of blocks from the turnoff to Roach Studios when I thought I heard a car horn.

"Jake, did that woman just honk at us?"

"What woman, Bambi?"

"The one driving that Buick that just went past in the other direction. I think she looked at us and honked."

"If so, I doubt if it was my good looks that caught her attention."

"You'd be wrong, Jake," she said, laying a hand on my right thigh.

"Now cut that out," I said, using my best Jack Benny take-off, and brushing her hand away.

The guard at the Hal Roach Studio, Mike Huse, recognized me and waved us through the gate toward a parking place, calling out, "Nice ride, Mr. Weaver!"

Bambi put my fedora back on my head as I parked, adjusting it just so.

At Roach's office, his secretary said that Hal was on Sound Stage Two directing an episode of the TV show *My Little Margie*, with Gale Storm, and that Rod

Serling was expecting me in the room just down the hall.

"Oh, could I go and see the *My Little Margie* scene?" Bambi pleaded. "I love Gale Storm."

The secretary said she didn't see why not, as long as she didn't enter the building when the red light was on and watched quietly in the background. Bambi promised and off she bounced, excitement in her steps. "I'll see you in half an hour, Jake," she called over her shoulder.

I found Serling sitting at a desk, hunched over a typewriter. He got up and said, "Jake Weaver, right? It's a pleasure. I've enjoyed your reports on CBS."

He was of average height, broad shouldered and had an open, expressive face, his hair and eyebrows thick and black. I said thanks and we shook hands. There was another chair beside the desk and I took it. A lit cigarette smoldered away in a half-filled glass ashtray.

"What are you working on there?" I asked, glancing at his typewriter.

"Trying to doctor up a script for *Trouble With Father*, one of Hal's comedies. It's pretty weak and Hal asked me to see what I could do. I've got an idea or two."

"That one stars Stu Erwin, doesn't it? My wife and I have seen it a time or two."

"That's right, Jake, Stu Erwin. A lot of not-quite stars or character actors from the movies, like Stu, have found new life in TV. Take Dick Lane for example. He was a hard-ass detective or something similar in the movies, never got top billing, and now he's a riot as a wrestling announcer on TV. He makes that fake wrestling fun. *Whoa, Nelly!*" Serling said, mimicking Lane's call when a wrestler gets slammed down on the canvas. He took a final drag on his cigarette and snuffed it out in the ashtray.

"I'm glad you're putting together a documentary on Hal and Mack Sennett," he went on. "Those early slapstick comedies were really something. It's swell that so many of them are being rediscovered these days in TV syndication. Laurel and Hardy are big stars all over again."

"Right," I agreed, "TV is hungry for content. The timing is good. Interest in those oldies has really picked up. Incidentally, Sennett's recovery is coming along well and he'll be able to leave the hospital pretty soon."

"Damn glad to hear it," Serling said. He gestured at his telephone and the wire leading from it. "One day," he said, "we'll all have little portable wireless phones that we carry around with us and these things will be obsolete."

"You think so?"

"Yes. I believe the required technology is just around the corner, or maybe two corners."

We talked a while about his projects, especially *Requiem for a Heavyweight*, and the anthology show he'd like to develop on paranormal occurrences. "A thing where people slip into a strange, other-worldly zone," he said. "Roach thinks I'm onto something there."

I wished him luck with that, then for some reason I mentioned the nightmares I sometimes had. He was easy to talk to.

"I have nightmares too," Serling said. "I get some ideas out of them, though. They're creative in an odd sort of way. Do you get ideas at night in your sleep?"

"Come to think of it, yeah, I do," I replied.

He offered me a cigarette, which I declined, and fired up one for himself. Then, echoing a thought I'd had for a few days now but hadn't wanted to admit to myself, he said, "Maybe that woman wasn't shooting at Mack Sennett at all. Maybe she was trying to kill *you*."

TWENTY-THREE

I drove Bambi back to her car at Columbia Square, didn't resist her quick kiss on the cheek, and headed for home.

The reason Rod Serling said the *woman* may have been firing at me was because the police were keeping it quiet that we thought the shooter was a man in disguise. That I might have been the target was a damn troubling thought as I cruised down Rossmore Avenue.

If that was the case, who'd want to kill me? The probable answer: some of Joe McCarthy's acolytes. His followers were die-hard idiots who believed his bullcrap no matter what proof sane journalists wrote and what Army investigators were providing in the current hearings. And these yahoos had seen my story exposing the man's lies.

Our craftsman-style house was eggshell-white with green trim. I reached it before Valerie did, and parked the Corvette at the curb in front rather than the driveway because Valerie liked to park in the garage. I'd move the 'Vet to the driveway later.

Inside, I fetched our bottle of Johnnie Walker Black Label, poured myself some, added two ice cubes and only a small splash of water. Man, I needed it.

The thought occurred that I should have gone up to the studio to check for messages after dropping off Bambi. Valerie might have called back after our brief conversation, seeking more details. Not being able to reach me would have been upsetting. I picked up my glass and gulped some scotch.

I replayed the depressing day in my mind. My poor old car. That woman who'd bumped it, saving my life. Being interviewed—damn it—for the network news, our local station, and the *Herald-Express*. Most of all, the feeling, underscored by Rod Serling's remark, that it was *me* that shooter might have been targeting.

After another hit on the Johnnie Walker, I heard Valerie's Plymouth Belvedere pull in, faster than usual, and screech to a stop in the driveway. That wasn't like her. I went out the side door to raise the garage door for her and got hit by a hurricane.

My wife had hopped out of her car, slammed the door, and punched me hard in the face with her right hand. "You bastard! You almost get killed and then go off joyriding around town in that hot car with some hot babe. Who the hell *are* you?"

My face stung but the words stung more. "Calm down, Val, take it easy and give a guy a chance to explain." I reached out and touched her arm. She flinched and backed away, but stopped after a step or two. Tears began to trickle down her face. She stared at me for a long moment but gradually inched forward. At last she let me put my arms around her. She leaned against me. "What am I going to do with you?" she said in little more than a whisper.

"I don't know, but next time Mickey Cohen challenges me to box, I'll have you pinch-hit for me. You've got a hell of a right there. You could take him."

That got the laugh I'd hoped for. It wasn't much of a laugh, just a soft chuckle but I was glad to hear it. "Come on, Val," I said. "Come in and have a drink with me and I'll tell you about my afternoon."

"Okay, and I'll tell you about *mine*! I'll park in the garage later. This had better be good." I tried to hold her hand as we went in. At first she pulled away but at last let me take it.

I fetched her a drink and we settled in the living

room, not side by side but facing one another, her on the sofa, me in an easy chair. She crossed her arms across her chest, never a good sign.

"Look, Val, I was a little shook up after that bombing—"

"A little?"

"Okay, Sweets, a lot shook up. Probably wasn't thinking straight. Anyway, I had an appointment with a guy at Hal Roach's, so I went out there. Maybe should've postponed, but I went. Took along my intern."

"I know." Valerie took a gulp from her glass. "Bambi, the journalism student, I assume?"

"That's right. How did you know?"

"Our friend Laurie Baker saw you, down near Culver City. She was going the other way. Said she honked at you."

"Hey, that's right. I didn't see her but Bambi did and said something about it." Laurie Baker had a big mouth. Should have minded her own business.

"Laurie says Bambi looked very pretty. You never mention Bambi's looks to *me*, Sailor." Said petulantly.

I took a drink. "Okay Val, yes, Bambi's an attractive young woman. She also happens to have a big talent for journalism. I'm hoping to get her a job after she graduates. I'm *not* lusting after her, and I'm sure as hell not going to jump her bones. And for sure we weren't joyriding yesterday. It was network business. I am doing a documentary, after all."

I wish she had said, "Okay I believe you," but instead: "When you called, I was in an important meeting with one of my bosses, a senior engineer, on a cooling jacket measurement problem, and couldn't talk long. I was frantic. When I had more time and called back later, Miss Morgan said you were out so I left a message asking you to call again. Didn't you get it?"

"Nope. After I dropped Bambi off I headed for home. I guess I should've gone up to the studio to check for messages, but just didn't. My mistake. I'm sorry."

I had to admit that her being a little threatened by Bambi kind of pissed me off. Here was Valerie, this beautiful, mature woman, surrounded by virtually nothing but men in her work environment. Some of them had to be young, good looking and, men being men, on the make. Did I ever show Valerie any concern or worry about that? No!

Even though I had some.

I reached up and touched the spot on my cheek where she'd clobbered me. It didn't smart much anymore but I wanted her to think it did.

Valerie took another drink, almost emptying her glass. "It's because I love you so much that I was so anxious," she said. "Needed to hear your voice, wanted more details."

At that point I refreshed our drinks, sat down again, and gave her details. The bomb squad, why the bomb went off prematurely, Detective Wannamaker, renting the Corvette, getting interviewed and becoming a news story myself.

"Tough day for both of us," she said. "You for going through it, me for worrying about you. Well, I'll go put my car in the garage now." Her tone was a little conciliatory. I hoped her mood would improve pretty soon. I went out and opened the garage door for her.

It was my turn to do dinner—we usually took turns—and of course I hadn't done a damn thing about that.

"Come on," I said. "I'm gonna take a hot babe joyriding, and then I'll buy her dinner." I locked up the place, took Valerie by the arm and steered her out to the Corvette. Got her seated, then jumped in the driver seat. "Best looking babe that's been in this car all day," I said, trying to work my best smile on her.

"Let's go to Perino's," I said as I pulled away from the curb. "One of our favorite places." We'd had some special times at this popular old restaurant on Wilshire.

"Okay, I guess, if that's you want." Her lack of enthusiasm was cutting.

"Take my hat if you would, Sweets. Don't want it blowing away."

As she reached up and took it, Valerie said, "Did Bambi hold your hat for you, too?"

I gritted my teeth and didn't answer. In fact, I held my tongue most of the way up to Wilshire.

"Nice car," Valerie broke the silence. "I suppose it has a top you can put up."

"It does, but I haven't tried it yet. The weather's so great today. I can put it up later when we're going home."

"Are you thinking of buying it?"

"Nah, it'll be a fun toy for a couple of weeks, but it's not my style. I'll get some kind of sedan when the insurance money comes in. You can help me pick it out."

When we arrived at Perino's, the greeter asked if we had a reservation. We hadn't. But the maitre d' recognized me and trotted over. "Ah, Mister Weaver, it's nice to have you and your missus with us tonight. Charles, show these people to table, uh, nine."

I'd become recognizable since joining CBS. My network reports often had me on camera. I wasn't comfortable with that, such a big change from my newspaper days, but once in a while it had its advantages. Like now.

The waiter named Charles showed us to a nice table. I scanned the wine list, then handed it to Valerie. "You decide, Sweets. What are you in the mood for?"

After a long moment of scrutiny she asked for the 1949 cabernet sauvignon.

Before it arrived and before we looked at the dinner menu, I said, "Theodore Bikel and Walter Slezak."

Valerie thought for a moment, then scrunched her nose and said, "Hmm. A pair of Austrian character actors? Close but no cigar, Sailor."

Calling me Sailor was a good sign, but I had to disagree with her. Bikel and Slezak were similar in looks and acting style and could easily play each other's roles. I didn't say so, because maybe her mood was starting to soften a little.

We ordered our meals, beef wellington for me and halibut for Valerie, but she quickly corrected herself: "Wait, no, cab doesn't go with halibut. Make mine a small filet, medium rare."

That settled, I said, "I met a guy down at the Roach studio today, a sharp young writer. He said maybe the person who shot Mack Sennett had actually been trying to hit *me*. Man, that gave me pause."

"Targeting you? Oh no, I hope not." Valerie reached over and touched my hand. "Someone tries to blow you up and then you hear that! I can't imagine having a worse day. Oh, Jake." A tiny tear began to form in her right eye. "My dear Jake."

She leaned back in her chair and said, "I guess I was fretting about my own feelings and not thinking of yours tonight because, well, I had a bad day, too."

"Really, Sweets? What happened?"

Before she could answer, the sommelier came with the wine. He uncorked the bottle and poured a little for Valerie to sample. She did the swirling and sniffing bit, gave her approval, and our glasses were filled.

We raised and clinked them, then she said, "That meeting I was in when you phoned, I was actually being called on the carpet."

"What? *You*?"

"It turns out I'd made a small measurement error on a cooling jacket."

"Cooling jacket?"

"Right, that jacket surrounds the combustion chamber and protects the outer part of the rocket from its great heat. It was the first time I'd ever made even the tiniest miscalculation, but in rocket design even small errors can't be tolerated. Fortunately one of my coworkers caught it, a young math whiz named Alex. We always double-check everything. But . . . ." Valerie stopped and a tear formed. She grasped and regrasped the stem of her wineglass nervously.

"But what?" I asked quietly.

Valerie pinched her lips, frowned, and then finally

said, "Alex said he would keep it between us if I'd sleep with him. This guy has always been coming on to me, and now this. I turned him down flat, so he went and told the supervisor in our section, hence the meeting and my getting chewed out."

"Any chance you might lose your job, Val?"

"No, just a stern warning to be more careful, never let it happen again, triple- and quadruple-check my figures from now on."

"No wonder you couldn't talk long on the phone," I said. "Had no idea."

"There's more," Valerie went on quietly. "True confessions time. Alex is a good looking guy with lots of personality. He'd been flirting quite a bit. One time and one time only—I'm not proud of this, Jake—we went into a storage room and made out a little. Some kissing and groping, just for a little while. I put a stop to it, wouldn't let it go any further."

I was pissed. This Alex creep made out with my wife and then ratted on her when a problem came up? Long-ago amateur middleweight that I was, I wanted to punch the guy's lights out.

"Do I feel guilty about this?" Valerie said. "Yes, of course, but I wanted to get it out there. I don't want to keep anything from you."

Suddenly I didn't feel bad about kisses with Bambi,

even though I hadn't instigated them.

I'd always trusted Valerie without question and this was a stunner. I knew that the future of our marriage might hang on what I said next. Be cool, I told myself. Aim for some tact and patience.

Our meals arrived, buying me a moment. The waiter served Valerie and then me.

Valerie picked up her steak knife, glanced at her filet, but then focused those deep blue eyes on me, waiting for me to say something.

Finally I said, "That was probably fun, Val, but it's good you stopped it when you did."

"That's it? You're not angry? You're not going to explode?"

Yeah, I wanted to, but what I managed to say was: "We've each been married twice, Val. We've both been around the block. We know that a little hugging and kissing can feel good. You had a moment of enjoyment but you didn't cheat on me. That's the big thing. You knew when to call a halt."

My lovely wife leaned across the table and laid both her hands on mine, a visible look of relief sweeping her face. "Sailor, you're the greatest. I don't deserve you."

"Well, that's true, you don't," I said, trying for a mischievous, disarming grin, "but you're stuck with me."

This disclosure revealed a side of Valerie I hadn't seen before. I guess we're all susceptible to our primal impulses from time to time.

Suddenly I didn't feel quite so guilty about having slept with a German woman, Gretchen Siedler, back in '42 during the war. Valerie and I weren't married at the time but we were engaged and the act had troubled me with a sense of betrayal. Maybe it shouldn't have.

As we slowly dug into our meals, Valerie said she was going to ask for a transfer so she wouldn't have to work with Alex the Judas anymore. "There's an opening in principal propulsion I could go for."

When the conversation drifted elsewhere, I felt kind of a perverse sense of validation and even pride, knowing that I'd landed a woman who other men found desirable, too. In fact, aware of other men's lust for Valerie made her all that more appealing to me.

She took a bite of salad, then said, "Jake, I know your mind is probably a whirlwind of emotions right now. Somebody trying to blow you up, me admitting to some extracurricular nuzzling which I never should have allowed, et cetera. So what else is going on down at CBS?"

"My intern Bambi thinks she and I should try to solve the Black Dahlia murder case."

"That grisly thing where somebody cut a young

woman in two? That's not a bad idea, Sailor. The police had a few leads, as I recall, but couldn't solve it. Doing this would be quite a feather in your cap."

"Make me a modern-day Sherlock Holmes, huh?" I took a small bite of my pâté-coated beef, put my knife down and said, "Well, maybe we'll give it a go. By the way, Bambi wants to invite us to her graduation. That's less than a month away."

During the rest of the meal we were quieter than usual. Was Valerie thinking she'd said too much and was beginning to regret it? We never really know what's going on deep inside someone else, do we? For my part, my mind was drifting back to who was trying to kill me with that car bomb. And was Rod Serling right that the shot that hit Mack Sennett might actually have been meant for me?

TWENTY-FOUR

It was a cool evening so I put the Corvette's top up for the drive home. Valerie said she appreciated that.

I was afraid I might have bad dreams that night, me getting blown to bits, Valerie indulging in a torrid, adulterous love affair, stuff like that. But when we crawled into bed, she snuggled, gave me an avid kiss with some tongue involved, and said, "Talk dirty to me." I nibbled on her right earlobe, and then whispered softly in that ear, "We're going to screw our brains loose." And that's what we did. Twice.

If I dreamed anything I couldn't remember it the next day.

Valerie said, "Wow," a couple of times in the morning, gazing into my eyes. "My brains are only now starting to tighten back up."

We just had coffee and Quaker Oats for breakfast. I didn't feel like cooking anything and neither did she. We each knew we faced a big day, Valerie possibly transferring to a different job at Lockheed while follow-ups from the bombing awaited me.

We didn't say much when we hugged goodbye but the eye contact and the closeness were more intimate than words.

After Bambi brought me coffee she leaned close and tried to kiss my lips, but I raised a hand to block it, saying, "Come on now Bambi, cool your jets there, huh?"

"I was just being affectionate," she said with a hurt look. "We work together so well."

We turned to the Black Dahlia murder. She and I sat at my desk, got out a fresh notebook and jotted down the names of the various suspects the police had investigated but never charged. We went over them one by one. I had to agree with Bambi that the doctor who'd fled to Hawaii, George Hodel, seemed the most likely culprit.

But I also wondered about Norman Chandler, publisher of the L.A. *Times*, who was tight with mobster Bugsy Siegel and who might possibly have gotten Miss

Smart pregnant. The *Times* had always been a big rival during my years with the *Herald-Express* and I wouldn't mind seeing it rocked by scandal.

"That Mark Hansen guy who owns the Florentine Gardens dance club might have done it," Bambi said. "Elizabeth Short lived in a house nearby that he owned, along with some other girls. It was sort of a dormitory for Hollywood wannabes. I figure maybe these gals serviced him in exchange for free rent. Maybe Short didn't want anything to do with that, so he took her out."

"But the police said his alibis checked out," I said.

"The cops did a sloppy job, Jake." Bambi nibbled on her yellow pencil. "You know they didn't even do a search of that house or even his car."

"Yeah, Detective Wannamaker told me the investigation was pretty slipshod. He said if he'd had the case he would have handled it better."

I looked at another suspect. "I'd like to put a big checkmark here beside the name of this surgeon from USC Medical, Dr. Walter Bayley, who specialized in female surgeries. Bayley's ex lived just a block from where Short's body was dumped. It had been a bitter divorce. Maybe he was trying to deliver some kind of sick message to his ex, like, 'See what can happen to unfaithful sluts?' "

"I'd hate for it to be him," Bambi said, "since he's dead. Says here he died back in '48. When we crack this, I want the culprit to be a live, breathing person. That'd make a far better story for us." I appreciated the way she said *when* we crack this, not *if.* Every day she was starting to sound more like a smart veteran newshound than a college J student.

After we turned briefly to Dr. George Hodel, the suspicious guy who vamoosed to Hawaii, I said, "The police notes say Short had a roommate for a while, before she moved into Mark Hansen's house. She lived with a woman named Ann Toth. The cops don't say anything more about her. I think we should try to find this Ann Toth person."

That was about all we could do that day. Bambi had classes that afternoon. "We'll take this up again in the morning," I said. "You try to find Ann Toth. I'll take on George Hodel, and think about how we might find what's going on with him in Hawaii."

She gave me a little kiss so quick I wasn't able to block it or turn away. "Gotcha, pardner," she said. "Gee, now you've got me using some of your Louisiana jargon." She collected her purse and skipped to the door, her gait both that of a little schoolgirl and yet sexy at the same time. I shook my head and asked myself what I was going to do with this saucy young lady.

I checked with New York and was told to put together something on the governor's upcoming wedding. Goodwin Knight, who was 58, was going to wed Virginia Piergrue, attractive widow of a World War II bombardier. She was 36, a full twenty-two years younger than "Goodie," as he was called.

Some people thought the age difference was indecent, a robbing of the cradle, but not me. I'd looked into Mrs. Piergrue and found her to be a solid citizen, a mother and Iowa native, with nary a hint of scandal to her name. I said if Goodie Knight, a widower for three years, had found someone nice to bring him comfort and share his life, good for him. So I told the brass that I'd gather information to be used at the time of the wedding in two months but that it wasn't a story now.

My mind went to my daughter Ilse and what she was up to with my friend Kenny Nielsen. Not knowing nagged at me. I also thought about my wife and wondered how her day was going, any repercussions from her error yesterday and the request for a transfer. And why the hell did Valerie tell me about necking with the very guy who ratted on her?

Miss Morgan stuck her head in the door and said, "You impress me, Mr. Weaver. Somebody tries to blow you to bits, and here you are carrying on just like nothing fazes you."

Little did she know.

That afternoon I met with my insurance agent, Herb Sands, who said my car was totaled—no surprise there—and after a little haggling we settled on an amount the company would pay. It would cover a new Chevrolet Bel Air, a rather sporty model I'd had my eye on for a while. I was in no hurry to go car shopping, though. I'd hang onto the rented Corvette and enjoy it for a few more days. Why not? CBS was paying.

The next excursion for this Corvette was to police headquarters downtown between Broadway and Hill, where Detective Wannamaker had summoned me to make my official statement about the bombing. I parked in the small lot behind the Romanesque sandstone edifice that was seriously showing its age. I hiked through echoing halls to the detective bureau located toward the front. I wondered how many thousands or millions of feet had trod this marble flooring before me. This old building was scheduled to be replaced in a year or two by the sparkling new Parker Center, still under construction.

Wannamaker himself wasn't there. My statement was taken by a young cop, Raymond Oliver, who was most likely an apprentice detective in training. His suit said J.C. Penney or Sears. We sat at a tattered wooden desk in a small office open to the hallway.

I told Oliver all I could remember about yesterday's occurrences and answered his questions as best I could. All the while, people passed by, their footsteps echoing in the hallway. When we finished, he asked me to wait while my report was typed up for my signature. Oliver left, gave his transcription to a typist somewhere I supposed, and came back. Out of curiosity I asked him where the files for open cases were kept and he said, pointing, "Just down the hall there, where it says Records."

The list of Black Dahlia suspects Bambi and I had been going over came from press coverage, mostly that of the *Herald-Express*. I'd always suspected that the police had soft-pedaled Norman Chandler as a suspect, even though he was known to have gone out with Elizabeth Short. The publisher of the *Times* had immense clout and was probably close to Police Chief William Parker. When Parker coined the term "the thin blue line" to characterize his department, Chandler gave it more play in the *Times* than it merited.

Against my better judgment I hiked over and opened the door marked Records. Sitting at the counter was a gray-haired guy probably in his 50s, chewing gum and reading a paperback. He looked up and said, "Can I help you?"

"Yes, I'd like to see the Black Dahlia case files." I was taking a big chance here, but I'd done that before.

"Are you a police officer?" he asked. I knew that files of open cases were available to any legitimate police, whether on the L.A. force or not.

"Yes, Dave Baxter, Santa Ana Police," I said, and flashed him the toy badge I'd bought at Woolworth's. This badge had worked for me before, as long as people didn't get a good look at it.

"Okay, Baxter," Gray Hair said. He led me down a short hall, around a corner and into a windowless room lined with metal filing cabinets and illumined by ceiling-hung fluorescent tubes. He examined one cabinet, then a second, and stopped at a third, where he pulled open a drawer and said, "Here we are. Hasn't been looked at in a long time." I wasn't surprised. While officially open, the case was now seven years cold. The guy handed me the file and motioned to a small desk at the end of the room. "Call out to me when you're done," he said. "I'll be able to hear you," and he left.

I sat in the cane-back chair, wiped some dust off the file and began going through it. The now-familiar names were there, including dance-club owner Mark Hansen; George Hodel, who'd scrammed to Hawaii; the physician Walter Bayley, and even to my surprise, the folksinger Woody Guthrie. All I found in that file was a note that said Elizabeth Short visited Guthrie in his dressing room after a concert to get his autograph. I shook my head—Guthrie wasn't known to be a womanizer.

The other files contained much more, lists of search warrants issued, tips received, typed-up notes on extensive interviews with both the suspects themselves and some of their acquaintances. I wiped some sweat off my forehead and looked behind me. I was still alone. So far, I was getting away with this.

The George Hodel file was incredible. At the time of the murder he was living with an ex-wife, a current wife and a common-law wife and five or six kids among the three of them. What an amazing polygamist. It was a wonder the women put up with him, a wonder that *he* wasn't murdered instead of Elizabeth Short.

I heard footsteps behind me and a tall cop appeared. Was I busted? The cop wore cowboy boots and a khaki uniform I didn't recognize. He stopped at a file cabinet close to me and opened a drawer. Looking over at me, he said, "How do?"and reached up to touch the brim of his Stetson. I nodded and answered, "Hello yourself."

"Raylan Givens, U.S. Marshall," he said and extended his hand, which I shook. "Based in Kentucky, out here on assignment."

"Dave Baxter, Santa Ana," I answered.

Givens extracted a thin file, closed the drawer and walked off. Whew! I wiped my damp brow and returned to George Hodel.

Maybe his move to Hawaii was so that he *wouldn't* be murdered by one of the women in his household. In the islands he married a Filipina woman from a wealthy family and fathered four more kids. How could a physician not believe in or know anything about prophylactics?

When I came to the Norman Chandler file, there was almost nothing, just a scant report from an investigating detective that said, "Subject Chandler admits to meeting and subsequently dating victim twice. States that she wasn't his type and had no further contact. No evidence to challenge assertion." That was it, no follow-through, no mention of any interviews with acquaintances of either Chandler or Short. Nothing!

That settled it for me. The police covered up for Chandler. Hell, he and Chief Parker probably played golf together at Riviera.

I was starting to jot this down in my notebook when footsteps thundered into the room and Gray Hair blurted, "You ain't no Santa Ana officer. I thought you looked familiar. Then I remembered, you're on TV. I seen you on the news. You're under arrest, fella. Criminal trespass! Impersonating an officer!"

TWENTY-FIVE

I was in a jail cell for the third time in four years. First time was in Switzerland, when a Zurich banker took his revenge on me, pulling strings with the local police he undoubtedly had in his pocket. Then it was in East Berlin after I'd been caught crossing into the communist zone without a pass, searching in vain for a kidnapped prime minister.

It was false arrest both times. This third time, though, was certainly *not* false arrest. I'd been caught red-handed impersonating a cop so I could look at some old crime files. Foolhardy! Stupid!

Trying to solve the Black Dahlia murder case wasn't

even my top concern at the moment. I'd let Bambi's enthusiasm for the project sway me. Number one, I needed to discover who tried to kill me with a car bomb. Number two, find out who tried to kill Mack Sennett, that is, if Sennett had been the target and not me. Number three, learn what my daughter Ilse was up to with my friend and coauthor Kenny Nielsen.

This was a small holding cell at police headquarters, not the main jail. It had rough sandstone walls, a standard iron-barred door and a battered wooden bench that had seen years of better days. The lack of a bunk and a commode meant that prisoners were only held here temporarily.

It was late afternoon. I should be out there checking on Valerie, seeing if my wife had gotten the transfer she wanted at Lockheed. Or preparing dinner at home waiting for her arrival. I could be cooking up some spaghetti or heating up some of the leftover meatloaf we had from a few days ago.

I slumped forward and put my head in my hands. I'd always been a risk-taker, but this one really took the cake, and I'd achieved almost nothing. I'd confirmed my hunch that the police had gone soft on *L.A. Times* publisher Norman Chandler in the Black Dahlia case, but there was nothing I could do with that. It was far too flimsy for me to do a story on it. It would look like

CBS was on a vendetta.

The gray-haired guard of the Records room had summoned a police sergeant who put me in here and said I'd be charged in a few minutes. Well, a few minutes had come and gone. I gazed around the cell. Some dates, names and initials had been carved in the sandstone walls. One name was Arne Bengtsson. Below it, someone had carved "Kilroy was here," that old prank that was popular during the war.

Occasional footfalls sounded in the hall, approaching, and then going past, and fading away in the distance.

I worried about what would happen if word of my arrest got around. Valerie would be pissed off with me: I had to go and get myself arrested on the very day when she had troubles of her own at work. The rival networks would have a field day. CBS might even fire me.

I leaned forward and put my head in my hands. The "few minutes" became a hell of a lot more.

At length, footsteps approached again. This time they didn't go on past. I looked up to see Detective Wannamaker and a uniformed cop march up to the bars.

"Well, lookee here," Wannamaker chortled. "It's the amazing Mr. Jake Weaver again! We find him and

Bela Lugosi over a dead body, we find him with a Nazi fugitive stabbing his daughter, we find him where his car's been blown to bits, and now this, we find him impersonating an officer so he can look at some files. Is there no place he isn't likely to show up?" He gestured to the cop. "Unlock this crazy guy."

"I thought we were supposed to write him up, sir."

"Forget it. We gotta get him outta here before he breaks the building down."

As I walked down the hall toward the exit with Wannamaker, he said, "Hell, Jake, if you'd only asked, I'd've showed you the Black Dahlia files. There's nothing secret about 'em.

"By the way, we found some fingerprints on your car, below the doors where there used to be running boards. That little strip of metal down there which you wouldn't be likely to touch but a guy crawling under your car would. We can check for matches in ours and the FBI's files of known criminal prints. That'll be time-consuming and a longshot, so don't get your hopes up, but I wanted you to know we'll be looking into it."

Valerie got home about an hour after I did. I'd heated up that leftover meatloaf, baked a couple of potatoes, and whipped together a green salad. Opened a bottle of pinot noir and poured a couple of glasses when I heard her car pull into the driveway.

After our hello hugs and kisses, Val kicked off her heels, took the glass of wine I offered, and sank onto the sofa.

I'd confess about my fiasco in the police records room pretty soon but first I wanted to know how her day went, if she got the transfer she was after.

The answer I got wasn't the one I wanted.

"I didn't ask for the transfer after all," she said. "I made it up with Alex, got him to promise to behave, and I'm staying where I am."

"But—" was all I got out before she cut me off.

"I'm learning a lot about rocket design where I am, and that's what I want. Principal propulsion would be a sideways move, almost a step back. I need to stay in design. That's where I've always wanted to be, in rocket design. That's the future and I have a need to be a part of it. I was stagnating in aircraft tool design at North American, you knew that, Jake. So please bear with me, back me up on this."

I didn't like this at all, her continuing to work with a guy who she was cuddling with and then ratted on her when she made a little mistake. Nope, didn't like it one bit. I thought that guy's promise to behave wasn't worth a damn.

I took a big sip of my wine before answering, but

finally said, "Of course I will, Sweets." My hesitation probably told her more than my words did. She was a savvy woman.

TWENTY-SIX

Over dinner I told Valerie about Detective Sergeant Wannamaker bailing me out of a possible arrest for impersonating an officer, the fingerprints the cops found on the remains of my car, what I'd learned about Black Dahlia murder suspects, and what I planned to do tomorrow.

We both tried hard to make it business as usual but the strain was palpable. I did appreciate, though, that her response to my near arrest was, "Oh Sailor, that's what I like about you, that you're so irrepressible." But she could have said love instead of like.

She also agreed with my surmise that the cops went easy on publisher Norman Chandler in their Black

Dahlia investigation because of his connections.

We hugged in bed that night but didn't make love. It was clear that the strain lingered. In spite of telling myself to knock it off, that I loved this amazing woman, I found myself not wanting to kiss or fondle her in the way that Alex guy might have done. That made me incredibly sad. It felt like a big stone was weighing down on my heart.

I had nightmares that night, I was pretty sure, but I couldn't remember them in the morning. Was glad of that. Breakfast with Valerie was pleasant, both of us trying hard to make it feel like old times but falling short.

I called Mount Sinai and found that Mack Sennett could be released today. I said that unless other plans had been made I would collect him and take him home. I called the office and told Miss Morgan I'd show up in late morning after fetching Sennett.

At the hospital, I parked in the patient pickup zone near the entrance while nurses steered Mack out in a wheelchair. He got to his feet carefully, using a cane, and lowered himself into the Corvette's passenger seat. A nurse handed me his bag of belongings, which I put in the back seat.

"Pretty sweet wheels you've got here, Jake," he said. Turning to the nurses, he added, "Thanks for everything, ladies. You've been swell."

On the ride to his home in Woodland Hills, he said the doctors thought he'd be okay at home but wanted him to have full-time nursing care for a while, which he'd arranged. A doctor would also check in on him every few days.

"I'll bet you're glad to be going home, pardner," I said.

"Damn right. The docs told me to take it real easy for a month or so. We don't want anything breaking open down there, but I'll be darn glad to recuperate in my own hacienda." When he again remarked on what a sharp car this was, I explained that it was a rental, that my Chevy had been blown up by a car bomb. He cried, "What! That worries the heck out of me, Jake."

When I told him how the bomb went off prematurely with me not in the car, he said, "Thank God for that."

I didn't mention the notion that I might have been the shooter's target instead of him outside the Brown Derby that day. But I told him about my visit to a hypnotist and that the thinking now was that the shooter was possibly a man disguised as a woman.

"Oh my God!" Mack uttered, and then fell quiet. He looked shocked.

"What? What are you thinking?" I asked him.

"Al St. John is skinny, has what you could call a rather feminine frame, and he hates my guts."

"Who's Al St, John?" I asked as I turned from Ventura Boulevard to Lankershim.

"Al worked for me in the old days, was one of the Keystone Kops at first, a very funny guy. I eventually moved him up to solo comedy roles. Slender fella. In the right clothes, clean shaven and wearing a wig, he could pass as a woman. He was a nephew of Fatty Arbuckle and a real close pal of his. Al and his 'Uncle Roscoe,' as he called him, were bosom buddies, practically joined at the hip.

"He blamed me for Fatty's downfall, said I detested his uncle. I have no idea where Al got that idea. Hell, I liked Arbuckle and he made me a lot of money. I had nothing to do with that stupid, tragic party in Frisco, nor any of the three trials that came afterward. Nevertheless Al still had it in for me."

I said I'd never heard of Al St. John.

"Well, you might have heard of Fuzzy St. John. Al grew a shaggy beard in the Thirties and reinvented himself as Fuzzy St. John, a cowboy sidekick. Kind of a poor man's Gabby Hayes. He even made sure his whiskers were cut just like Gabby's."

"Okay, *that* I remember," I said. "How old is this

guy?"

"I'd say early sixties, Jake. He was born just before the turn of the century. He was a sidekick to Buster Crabbe in some B westerns. He could have been the guy who shot me, I wouldn't be surprised. Say, I wonder if Al knows anything about making a car bomb?"

Damn good question, I thought. "You going to pass this suspicion on to the cops?" I asked.

"Sure, next time they question me."

I helped him out of the car when we arrived at Sennett's house. I supported his left side and he used a cane as we tottled to the door. He said the caregiver he'd arranged for would arrive sometime that morning. I decided to go inside with him and write some notes while we waited. Al "Fuzzy" St. John, a Keystone Kop who became a Western sidekick character, would become a part of my documentary, albeit a small one, whether he turned out to be the shooter or not. I too wondered if Al St. John knew how to make a car bomb.

Mack settled in an easy chair, put the cane aside, and looked around the room with a smile on his face, clearly happy to be home. I fetched him a glass of water from the kitchen. After I took a seat on the couch, I told him I'd like to get some Al St. John footage for my documentary. He said I could get the Keystone Kops stuff from the Film Preservation Society and film from the "Fuzzy" days from the PRC studio, which had produced a lot of those B westerns.

Before long the caregiver showed up, a gray-haired nurse, outfitted in appropriate white and probably in her late forties. After the introductions, she made the rounds of the house, familiarizing herself with the various rooms. Knowing that Mack was in good hands, I took my leave. He said, "Thanks for everything. Now let's keep in touch. Let me know if you find out anything more about that car bomb."

I said, "I sure will, you big Canuck," and headed for Columbia Square.

When I arrived at the office, Bambi bounded up and—after looking around to make sure Betsy Morgan wasn't nearby—tried to kiss me hello. But I turned my head and threw up a hand in defense. Bambi said, "Aw," and gave me a pouty look. But she quickly brightened and said she'd been looking into two of our Black Dahlia suspects.

"You're really excited to be a journalist, aren't you, Bambi?" I said. "You should meet my daughter Ilse, a reporter with the Pasadena *Star-News*. You'd have a lot in common. She wants to be the next Nelly Bly."

"Nelly Bly?" Bambi asked.

"Nelly was the first great woman reporter," I

explained. "Started off with the Pittsburgh *Dispatch* and then moved up to Joseph Pulitzer's *New York World.* Real name was Elizabeth Cochran but she made Nelly Bly her pen name. She had herself committed to a New York lunatic asylum to expose the ghastly conditions there. She also traveled around the world in less than eighty days to break the record of Jules Verne's fictitious Phileas Fogg. Quite an accomplishment in 1890. She even stopped in France to meet Verne during her journey."

"Wow, what a role model," Bambi said. "Thanks for telling me about her. As to meeting Ilse, I'd like to do that just after graduation. That's in less than two weeks now. You and your missus better be there! I got two tickets for you. Now, Ilse was born in Germany, is that right."

"Yes, I was there in 1930 for the memorial service for my Aunt Marta, who'd just passed away. I met a lovely woman, Winifrid, and, well, things developed kind of fast."

"You rogue, you," Bambi smirked. "So you stayed in Germany for a few years?"

"No, I came back home to Loozanna, had no idea Winifrid was pregnant. She never wrote to tell me. So, long story short, the Gestapo found out she was anti-Nazi, killed her in a concentration camp, and threw Ilse into an orphanage. I didn't know anything about Ilse till 1942 when she was twelve. That was when I snuck into Nazi Germany for FDR—I've told you about that. Anyway, we managed to scram out of that madhouse together and she did the rest of her growing up here. Can't tell you how proud of her I am."

"I can't wait to meet her, Jake. I can see her becoming my big sister."

"That'd be swell, darlin'," I said. "Now before you dig back into the Black Dahlia, I'd like to find out what you can about a minor movie actor named Al St. John."

"Sure, Jake. How come?"

"He might've been the guy who shot Mack Sennett."

Bambi made a "wow" shape with her lips and loped off to her desk.

I called the cop shop and asked for Detective Sergeant Wannamaker. He wasn't in so I left a message: You might want to get the fingerprints of a Western actor named Al St. John.

Then Miss Morgan came in with the daily news budget from New York. President Eisenhower, speaking to Washington reporters, warned of a possible communist domino-effect in the Indochina area. The Army-McCarthy hearings were close to conclusion. The newly christened Baltimore Orioles, who were the St. Louis Browns last year and the fifty years before that, were looking for their fifth win.

I felt Miss Morgan staring at me while I read. "Something's wrong, isn't there, Mr. Weaver?" she said at last. "I see in your face that you're a little off. Is it something at home?"

"You're too savvy by half, Betsy," I said.

"Give her a dozen of the reddest roses you can find and tell her you love her more than anything!" this woman commanded. "No excuses now."

I stopped at a florist on the way home to follow that sage advice. I also picked up some chocolates at a candy store and got some chicken enchiladas for dinner at a Mexican takeout. Man, my hands were full when I walked up to our front door. The garage door was closed and the driveway was empty so it looked as if Valerie wasn't home yet.

I set the flowers and candy box down and juggled the enchilada sack in my left hand while I slid my key in the front-door lock. To my surprise it wasn't locked. I nudged the door open with my foot and picked up the flowers and candy.

There stood Valerie in the middle of the front room, holding a glass of white wine. When she saw me, she put her glass down on the coffee table and rushed up to take the roses, saying, "Sailor, these are gorgeous.

Thanks so much." She held them to her face and took a deep sniff. "And candy too. What's the occasion?"

"No occasion, Sweets, just that I love you. A lot." I went into the dining room and set the enchiladas on the table. Val followed, put the roses down there too and said, "I'll put these in a vase but first . . ." She threw herself into my arms and planted her A-Number One Kiss on my mouth. Mmm.

When we pulled away from the embrace, she said she'd pour me a glass of wine and dashed off to the kitchen. I went into our bedroom to take off my hat and suit coat. Val's suitcase sat in the middle of our bed. That stopped me in my tracks! Looked like it had been packed.

What the hell?

TWENTY-SEVEN

A moment later Valerie appeared with a glass for me. "It's that chardonnay we like," she said.

I took the glass, gestured at the suitcase and said, "You going somewhere?"

"Actually, yes. To White Sands, New Mexico, to see your old friend Wernher von Braun test launch a Redstone rocket. This opportunity came up suddenly, a real surprise. We don't make the Redstone, of course, but they're happy to have us observe."

I had found von Braun trying to evade the Gestapo in the foothills of the Alps in 1945 and got him into Allied hands, hence her "old friend" remark. It was basically just luck but the British gave me a nice award for the exploit. I'd interviewed the famous rocket engineer twice since, at White Sands, before he went to Huntsville, Alabama to set up the Redstone Arsenal there.

I was full of worry—and questions. "How long will you be gone?" I asked.

"A couple of days."

"When do you leave?"

"Right away, in the morning. We fly Western Airlines to El Paso."

"Who all is going?"

"My supervisor and a couple of others."

I was afraid one of the "others" would be Alex, the guy who'd made out with her and then ratted on her over the small error she'd made.

"It was a surprise and rather sudden invitation," Valerie went on. "At this point the top three missiles in our young space program are our Viking, the Atlas, and the Redstone. Getting to see the Redstone perform is a great opportunity."

"Von Braun's got an ego," I said. "Wants to show off to you guys. If you get to meet him, tell him you're my wife and that I said hi."

"I surely will. Now let's dig into those enchiladas."

Over dinner it came out that Alex indeed would be a member of Lockheed's traveling party tomorrow. "It's nothing to worry about," Valerie insisted. "I put him in his place and he's minding his p's and q's now."

I wanted to say, "But you're the rookie, and these guys are your mentors, the ones you need in order to expand your rocket knowledge, and that puts you in a position of vulnerability." But I didn't. Couldn't. Tried to be as pleasant and positive as I could through dinner and afterward. I knew I was faking it, and was pretty sure she did too.

"I'll drop you at the airport in the morning," I said.

"Thanks, hon, but they're sending a company car. They'll pick me up right here."

As I lay awake that night I thought back to some of the tropical storms that used to lash Baton Rouge when I was a kid. Some of them were doozies. They would roll in from the Gulf of Mexico, sweep across the swamps of the Atchafalaya Basin and draw a bullseye on us. Lightning would flash like a fireworks show, thunder rumble its deep bass notes, fierce gusts of wind slap tree branches against our windows sounding like shrieks. All of this frightened six- or seven-year-old me. Scared the bejeezus out of me.

My mother would comfort me, brushing my forehead with a soft hand and saying, "This storm will pass, son, they always do. Tomorrow will be dry and sunny, you'll see." She was usually right. Often I would see a rainbow in the morning and wonder about the pot of gold that was supposed to be at its base.

I tried to find solace in my mom's words right then. I knew that my marriage had run into some stormy weather. I wanted to believe it would pass and evolve into dry and sunny. That was my hope as I eventually fell asleep. I couldn't say if I had dreams or nightmares.

In the morning I wished Valerie a good trip. "Should be a fine experience for you, seeing the Redstone and all. Hope you get to talk with von Braun."

When a horn tooted, she gave me a quick peck on the lips, hurried to the door and toted her bag out to the curb. I didn't go to the window and look. I didn't want to glimpse the men in that car. Maybe one of them was a look-alike for Errol Flynn or Tyrone Power.

I looked at the dozen roses, seated now in a vase of water. They'd wilt a bit but still look okay when Valerie got back. I was tempted to grab the damn things and toss them in the trash. But didn't.

I plunked myself down at the kitchen table and poured myself a second cup of coffee. Glanced through the *Morning Examiner* lying there. A story on page three caught my eye: TV newsman Everett Hensley was let go by NBC here. The story didn't say but I'd heard he'd been drinking heavily. I didn't especially like the guy I'd beaten out for this job, but I hated to see anyone's career get derailed. Poor guy.

Then I recalled that a big dinner was coming up to honor company founder Alan Lockheed. I was sure to meet Valerie's boss and her coworker Alex. Wasn't looking forward to *that*.

When I got to the office I decided to spend most of my time on the documentary. I'd been neglecting it lately, distracted by the car bombing, the shooting of Mack Sennett, the Black Dahlia, Bambi's infectious enthusiasm, and of course my relations with Valerie.

I asked Bambi to contact the Film Preservation Society and PRC to see if CBS could borrow some Al St. John footage, the former from his silent-film roles and the latter from his days as a cowboy sidekick. While saying this, I purposely stood several feet from her, backing away if she came forward. I wanted her to get the message: no kissing.

I turned to my documentary. I needed to organize my voluminous notes into a timeline, starting with Mack Sennett, then Hal Roach. The first two dozen pages of my notebook were filled with items I'd scribbled down while talking with Sennett, Roach, Rod Serling and others.

I began to sketch out my timeline on a fresh page.

Started with Sennett's birth in Canada, his early filmmaking in New York, and founding his Keystone Studios in L.A. in 1912. Then the Keystone Kops and the first pie-throwing comedies, his years with Charlie Chaplin, Mabel Normand and Bing Crosby, and of course the Roscoe Arbuckle tragedy. I would include how "Stone Face" Buster Keaton co-wrote and co-directed a film with Arbuckle in 1917.

I paused at Mabel Normand's name. Sennett had told me that the lovely star had been his one true love and that not marrying her was the biggest regret of his life. Should I include that in the documentary? I bit at the end of my pencil pondering the question. After cogitating for a few moments I decided that I would. It might embarrass or even anger Mack but it was a poignant fact, one that viewers would find touching.

I called my secretary over and ran those pros and cons by her. "Betsy, do you think I made the right call?"

She scrunched her lips a moment, thinking, then said, "Yes, Mr. Weaver. It's touching, very human. Your viewers will be moved by it."

Did I see a small tear forming in one of her eyes as she turned her head away? Had she had a similar disappointment in her life? Instead of going there, I said, "Thanks, Betsy. Don't you think you could call me Jake?"

When she was gone, Bambi rustled over to report that we could get the desired Al St. John film as long as we credited the source. "We always do," I said. "Good work, y'all. If you have time before going to school, see if you can find face shots of Mabel Normand, Marie Dressler and Buster Keaton." I spelled the names for her, making sure she had a "d" at the end of Normand's last name. "Start locally. KNX may have them or the network. You'd have to telex New York for that."

I double-checked that I had the Mack Sennett chronology set down correctly, then turned to Hal Roach, starting on a fresh page.

First, his birth in Elmira, New York, followed by prospecting for gold and briefly being a mule skinner. Audiences would appreciate his "untamed youth" days. Then his first attempt at acting, which by his own admission was a big flop. Forming a studio in 1914 to make films with his talented friend Harold Lloyd. Founding the more successful Hal Roach Studio in Culver City five years later. Clashes with Lloyd and the rupture of their partnership. First working with Will Rogers in 1923. The popular and lucrative Our Gang Comedies (called The Little Rascals these days in TV syndication). His hugely successful and profitable work starting in 1925 with Stan Laurel and Oliver Hardy. Roach's early use of Jean Harlow and Boris Karloff. His later success in talkies with the likes of Cary Grant and Constance Bennett, and nowadays of course, television.

I felt that it was coming together pretty well. There were funny, poignant and fascinating things to say about each man and his career, and the same could be said for many of their stars. I hoped to have a good mix of film clips, still shots, and face shots. If the case was solved in time, near the close I could bring up the attempt on Sennett's life. Or maybe start with that? I'd have to think on that some more.

Interviews with each man still needed to be filmed and a narrator found. I hoped the network wouldn't insist I narrate it myself. I'd been thinking of Douglas Fairbanks Jr. or maybe Francis X. Bushman. Neither had any real connection to Sennett or Roach but both were big names and had distinctive voices. Bushman had been a major star in silent dramas, including *Ben-Hur*. I even thought for a moment about young Rod Serling. He was an unknown but had a resonant, rather captivating voice.

It was Friday. The Redstone launch demonstration would take place today, and then tomorrow the Army would host some dinners and events for their guests. Clearly, the military-industrial complex that President Eisenhower had warned against was underway. On Sunday Valerie would return.

TWENTY-EIGHT

I decided to use the Saturday for car-buying. The insurance money hadn't come in yet, but I had the itch. I dropped the Corvette off at Hertz and cabbed it to Felix Chevrolet on South Figueroa, where I met with Winslow Felix, an old contact from my *Herald-Express* days. That huge Felix the Cat sign stood above the office, probably the second-most known sign in the area after the famous Hollywood Sign.

"After that car bomb, I figured I'd be seeing you one of these days," Felix said. "Thank God you weren't killed." I'd bought the now destroyed hulk here four years ago.

He tagged along while I looked over several models.

He asked me if the cops were going to find out who shot Mack Sennett and what was I working on these days. I answered as best I could, meanwhile deciding the Bel Air sedan was for me. Chose a white one and took it for a test drive, Felix riding along. As I turned from Figueroa to Grand, he said, "This model goes for $1,850, but for an old friend who's now a TV star I'll knock off two hundred bucks."

Passing the Olympic Auditorium, I replied, "That's a deal, pardner, thanks." I took my right hand off the wheel and we shook on it. "This baby handles real swell," I said, "I'm gonna like it."

Back at the dealership, we did the paperwork in his office, me deciding on the car radio, white sidewall tires and leather upholstery. I signed, wrote a check for the whole amount, and asked him not to deposit it till Tuesday. I explained that I didn't have the necessary balance in my checking account, but would move funds from my savings account on Monday to cover it. Once I got my check from the insurance company I'd be solvent again.

I thanked Felix and drove off with my new wheels, enjoying the new-car smell. The Bel Air didn't have the Corvette's flash but it suited me fine. I had the rest of Saturday to myself so I said why not see a movie before heading home. Decided on *Brigadoon* at the Egyptian

Theatre in Hollywood. I appreciated the ornate detailing in that place, its stage surrounded by carved columns and models of the Sphinx.

I mostly enjoyed the musical fable about an enchanted village in Scotland. The Lerner and Loewe songs were lively and catchy, Gene Kelly was good, Cyd Charisse gorgeous as always, but I found Van Johnson clumsily overplaying the heavy.

As I drove away in the new car I found myself singing, "Go home, go home, go home with Bonnie Jean." Before going home, going home, I stopped for Chinese takeout at the Formosa Café.

I was lonely that Saturday night. The house felt quiet and empty without Valerie. I called Ilse in Pasadena to see if my daughter could come over and share some chow mein with her *Vati*. There was no answer. She was probably out with friends; not with Kenny Nielsen I hoped.

It would be nice if Valerie would call and tell me how it was going out there, but she didn't. I thought about phoning somebody about going out for a drink, maybe Marko Janicek, my old newspaper pal. Even thought of Bambi, but just for an instant. Forget that, I told myself. I watched *The Jackie Gleason Show* on TV and went to bed early.

I scrambled some eggs in the morning and

had them with toast and coffee. Read the morning papers. Not much news. In Indochina, French forces were struggling against Vietminh rebels led by a guy named Ho Chi Minh. In sports, Ben Hogan and Carey Middlecoff shared the lead in the Houston Open, and the Hollywood Stars beat the Oakland Oaks.

In midafternoon I was jotting down notes about my documentary. One of my next steps was to schedule my filmed interviews with Sennett and Roach. I wanted to book at least an hour for each. Afterward, we'd edit it down to just the best parts. My new Chevy was in the driveway, Valerie's Plymouth Belvedere in the garage, where it had been for three days.

That was when I heard a car pull to the curb and a door slam, followed by footsteps approaching the house. I opened the door for Valerie, who looked back and waved at the car, then came in toting her suitcase, looking both tired and excited.

She set the bag down and hugged me, saying, "Hiya, Sailor, bought yourself a new car, I see." She pulled away, took her things to the bedroom and came right back. Before I could ask how it went, words began to tumble from her mouth.

"Gosh, it was really something, Jake. The Redstone launch went perfectly! Von Braun is such a gentleman. The Army treated us like royalty. You should have seen the dining room. The weather was grand. The Redstone's very impressive. I'm afraid it's ahead of the Atlas and our Viking. I'm so glad to be in rockets. How was your weekend? Oh, the big dinner they threw for us on the base there. Fine wines, several cuts of meat. Von Braun says hello. Big handsome man, isn't he? How do you like the car?"

I held up a hand. "Whoa there, slow down, Val."

She took a deep breath and sank onto the sofa. "Could you get me a drink?" she asked.

I fetched a couple of glasses and poured in some Early Times, a splash of water, a few ice cubes, and handed one to her. We clinked glasses, said "Cheers," and imbibed.

"What do you mean when you say the Redstone is ahead?" I asked.

"In the race to put an artificial satellite in orbit. That's what we want to do, and so do the Russians. I've told you this before. That Redstone Arsenal is getting tons of money from the Army while we and General Dynamics are basically on our own."

I didn't tell her I was sure Lockheed and GD would soon be getting big government contracts too. Instead, I asked about the parties and the lodging, et cetera. She said they stayed at El Paso's finest hotel, which was nice but not up to L.A. standards, and that the dinner and other events were held at the White Sands base, seventy miles away.

"The launch was thrilling," she said. "We watched through a thick window in a concrete-block bunker about a quarter mile from the launch pad. There was one hold in the countdown because of some kind of problem, but after that was squared away the count continued on down. Two. One. Ignition. Liftoff. A flood of orange-red flame burst from the engines and the rocket began a slow climb, then got a little faster, faster yet, and pretty soon swept up into the sky. They say it attained an altitude of about 35 miles."

I said I wished I could have seen that, then asked if von Braun's wife Maria Luise was there. "No, I guess she was back at Huntsville. Wernher said he remembers you well and wishes you the best. He's quite the flirt. He kissed my hand, also my cheek and said you didn't deserve such a lovely wife."

But I do, don't I? I thought but didn't say. "Yeah, he's a charmer," I managed.

She went on and on about the events, the flights (a little bumpy coming back over the San Jacinto Mountains) and so on. I asked if her male colleagues in the party had a good time too, and she said sure without elaborating.

When at last she wound down, I told her about the car, which she simply said looked nice.

I took some pork chops from the fridge, fried them and pieced together a salad while Valerie unpacked and changed into lounging clothes.

She was so spent from her three-day jaunt that she could hardly eat her meal. We talked for a while afterward but not long. I could see she was just too tired. I don't think it registered at all when I told her about seeing *Brigadoon*. We turned in early. No hanky-panky.

In the morning, Valerie busied herself cooking sausages and eggs, maybe trying to make amends for the distance she'd allowed to emerge between us the last few days? I hoped that was it.

While I tended to coffee and toast, she asked, "What are you up to today, Jake?"

"Working on my documentary, hoping to schedule the one-hour interviews I need to film with Sennett and Roach. I'd also like to set one up with Lillian Gish. She's still alive and kicking. She and Sennett briefly worked together when they were both at Biograph Studios. That was before Keystone. First, though, I'll stop at the bank and transfer some money from savings to my checking account so the check I wrote for the car Saturday will be good."

"How much do you need to cover it, Sailor?"

"Nine hundred bucks should do it. Now what's on your slate for today, Sweets?"

"We'll do a little postmortem on what we learned at White Sands, what the Redstone has that our Viking series lacks, and then brainstorm ideas on how we can close the gap."

Our goodbye kiss and hug was the best in several days, but still not as warm and fulfilling—or so it seemed to me—as BSWA (Before Smooching with Alex).

TWENTY-NINE

I walked the two blocks from Columbia Square to First Federal Bank, arriving just after it opened. Instead of going to a teller, I went to see the branch manager, Tony Adriano, an old friend.

He offered me coffee, which I declined. "Tony," I said, "I need to move nine hundred dollars from my savings over to checking. Bought a car Saturday and the check I wrote's a little short."

"That's already been taken care of, Jake."

"Whatta you mean, Tony?"

"Your wife called ten minutes ago and moved nine hundred of her funds to your checking account."

"Fr- from *her* account?" I stammered. "Well I'll be

damned."

"Right. We normally don't allow such transactions over the phone, Jake, but I trust such good customers as you and your missus. Here's the transfer slip. Why don't you just forge her signature for me and put your own John Hancock on the deposit slip?"

I'll be a monkey's uncle, I said to myself as I hiked up the street. Out of her own account! That gesture sent quite a message. That was the kind of thoughtful thing Valerie used to do back when we were first a couple. I'd have to be sure and pay her back. I was in a good mood as I took the elevator up to my office.

Bambi had finals the next two days so I had the place to myself. Betsy Morgan brought me coffee, saying, "For once that eager beaver didn't beat me to it." I grinned at that and asked her to see if she could locate Lillian Gish for me.

Then I set about scheduling interviews for my documentary. Sennett was recovering at home so it was easy to set it up for there for this afternoon. Roach said he could do it tomorrow morning. I arranged for a sound guy and a cameraman to accompany me at both.

Pretty soon Miss Morgan came in and said, "I located Miss Gish's personal manager. He tells me she lives in her apartment in Manhattan." I had assumed the aging actress lived in the L.A. area. I'd have to get the home office to do the interview. Ed Murrow would do a fine job if he was interested. So would Charles Collingwood.

I started a list of questions for whoever took on the job. The lovely young Lillian Gish had preceded Mary Pickford as "America's Sweetheart." Never married, she had been close to D.W. Griffith back in the day. It was rumored they'd been lovers. It would be delicate, but maybe all these years later she would let me know if that were true.

I'd also like to ask about her anti-war stance before Pearl Harbor. She had been an ardent supporter of Charles Lindbergh and the America First Committee, which had a good opinion of Hitler and mocked FDR's support of Britain. She and everyone else changed their tune after Pearl Harbor. This would just be a sidebar, though. A lot of people had wanted to keep us neutral. After all, the documentary was about the slapstick days and I'd mainly want her to talk about the comedies that she'd been in, not her politics.

I called Sig Mickelson, our boss, brought up the Gish interview and asked if Murrow could do it. "Why don't you come and do it yourself?" he said, surprising the heck out of me. "Spend a day or two with us and get reacquainted with everybody, Fred Schoenbrun, Walter Cronkite, the whole gang. This is Monday.

Fly here Wednesday and go back home Friday. We'll schedule Miss Gish for Thursday. I'll set it up myself."

I hadn't been in New York since my orientation last year when I was hired, so I readily agreed, thanked him, and hung up, walking on air. What next? Oh yeah, helping Bambi to get a job.

I had approached the news director of our local affiliate, KNX, about hiring her halftime as a rookie reporter while we, the network, took her for the other half, splitting the salary. I went to see him again and found that he'd got that approved. As I already had CBS's okay in my pocket, it was now a done deal. Bambi had a paying job here after graduation, which was just days away.

What a damn fruitful day I was having!

I asked Miss Morgan to call the airlines and book flights for me.

After a quick lettuce and ham sandwich in the KNX cafeteria, I was off to my filmed interview with Mack Sennett. We had him sit in a chaise longue on his patio as it was a warm, sunny afternoon, his nurse and I helping him out there while my cameraman set up.

As I went through my list of questions, he volunteered some items that I hadn't uncovered yet, such as the fact that his early sketches were often copied from British music hall routines. He noted that he was the first to take cameras outdoors for better scenes and more action; at Biograph, D.W. Griffith had always worked in studios, which was limiting.

Mack responded warmly and cordially, that is, until I got to Mabel Normand. "Breaking it off with Mabel was the biggest mistake of my life," he uttered, his head starting to hang a little. "If only I could have that day over." His eyes grew watery. "She made me so happy and then I had to go and . . ." He stopped midsentence, shook his head slowly and said, "Do you have to use that?"

"I don't know, Mack. Maybe not." It would be a tough call but I *did* want to use it. It would provide some poignancy in my film.

That evening I thanked Valerie for moving money into my checking account, saying the surprising and sweet gesture meant a lot to me. When I told her I'd pay her back when the insurance money arrived she said not to worry about it. Meanwhile, she whipped up a chicken enchilada casserole, which we enjoyed with some Dos Equis beer.

I described the Sennett interview and asked her opinion of my using his regrets about dumping Mabel Normand. Her answer was the same as my secretary's: use it, it's very touching.

After telling her how tasty the casserole was, I sprang the news of my New York trip. She was surprised but supportive. "It'll be good for you to rub elbows with the brass," she said. "I'll keep the home fires burning." In the back of my mind, I couldn't help but fret about what fires she would actually be burning.

That night I had a nightmare. It wasn't the usual one with a gunshot coming at me. I dreamt that Valerie was walking away from me, down a long corridor. The passageway grew narrower and narrower and she was getting smaller and smaller the farther she got. I tried to run down that corridor and catch up to her but just couldn't. It felt like my feet were stuck in molasses.

In the morning I kept the troubling dream to myself, not a word about it to Val.

After she left for work, I called Bambi and told her I'd be in New York the rest of the week after first interviewing Hal Roach today at his studio. I wished her well in her finals and reminded her that after they were completed she was to be looking for a photo of Mabel Normand and also trying to find Ann Toth, who'd been a friend of the Black Dahlia victim. "Will do, Chief," she said breezily. "Have fun in the big city." I'd give her the good news about her new job here after I got back.

Roach and I talked on a well-lit sound stage, seated in canvas director's chairs. Before we started, he asked how Sennett was doing and was happy to hear my report. When we got rolling he spoke of their rivalry for talent and their artistic differences. "I copied Mack at first but then went in for lengthier gags, more carefully constructed. His were more slam-bam. I went in more for character than non sequitur. I wanted people to care for my actors, not just see them as buffoons. You couldn't root for a Keystone Kop but you could for a Stan Laurel."

Reminded that both of them used pie-throwing scenes, Hal said, "Yes, but Mack's were thrown willy-nilly, just plaster everybody and everything. Mine were thrown with greater accuracy," he added with an impish grin.

I saw no need to go into his brief, fruitless business venture with Vittorio Mussolini.

Answering a question, he said he'd been lucky in love. He'd married an actress, Marguerite Nichols, in 1916. She died in 1941 after twenty-five happy years. Then he'd married Lucille Prin, whom I met at his home the other day, "and hit the jackpot there, too."

Wait a minute! At his home the other day when I asked about his relations with Constance Bennett in the '30s, he winked and said he wasn't married at the time. But he'd just confided that he *was* married then, and was until 1941. I decided to let it go. No need in my documentary to sully the reputation of a man who was alive and still active in filmmaking.

At home that night I told Valerie I was happy with both interviews and I'd start editing them down to the good stuff when I got back from New York. In turn, she told me about her day, saying nothing big occurred, mostly just some study of various propellant fuels and oxidizers.

In the past whenever I'd flown east or to Europe, Val had driven me to the airport and invariably said, "You'd damn well better come back to me." This time she wasn't able to because she had an early meeting at Lockheed, so I'd drive and leave my new car in the airport parking lot.

Before I left she hugged me tightly and said, "Good luck, Sailor. You'd damn well better come back to me." Ah, she remembered! That was a good sign and it gave me a warm feeling as I headed off to Inglewood and the former Mines Field, now rebranded as Los Angeles International Airport and mushrooming with new construction.

Betsy Morgan had been able to book me on one of United Air Lines' new nonstops to New York on a Douglas DC-7, arriving at Idlewild Airport in the Jamaica section of Queens in a little over seven hours. This was a big improvement over previous flights that usually required fueling stops in places like Denver or Chicago.

I took along John Steinbeck's new novel, *Sweet Thursday*, a sequel to his *Cannery Row*, which I'd enjoyed a great deal, as well as my documentary notebook and list of questions for Lillian Gish.

As was normal, the plane took off into the westerly winds, crossing Dockweiler Beach and over the ocean before circling back to the east. I looked out from my window seat at the L.A. basin sprawling below, the Hollywood Sign, and the San Gabriel and San Bernardino Mountains. I was able to identify Mount San Antonio, better known by its nickname, Mount Baldy, and then the regal San Gorgonio, king of Southern California's mountains.

I accepted coffee from a stewardess and when we got over desert terrain I turned to the book. After about four chapters, I dozed a while, then was served lunch. I chatted a bit with the man seated next to me, an executive with Mobil Oil. Looked down on flat Midwestern farm land and rivers. Then came another nap. When we approached New York it was after dark and the lights were dazzling, except for two black ribbons which had to be the Hudson and East Rivers.

Douglas Edwards, our chief anchor, met me at Idlewild. Damn nice of him.

He drove me to the Berkshire Hotel at 52nd and Madison Avenue, not far from CBS Broadcast Center. After checking in I had a drink with Doug at the hotel bar. He said I was to meet with the "news gang"at 9 in the morning and my Lillian Gish interview was set for 10:30 in her apartment.

At the meeting in the a.m., I described my documentary and other projects, including the Black Dahlia. Sig Mickelson and Douglas Edwards said I was doing a fine job and to keep up the good work, which had me popping my buttons.

Walter Cronkite offered a good suggestion, saying I should try to be more relaxed and natural on camera. I said, "Thanks, Walt. Still new in this business, I know I'm a little self-conscious on the air."

"I felt the same thing when I first left the *Houston Press*," he said.

He and the others tossed several questions at me. They were mostly about the Mack Sennett shooting, Mack's recovery, and whether the cops were making progress. I described my hypnosis experience and said we now thought the shooter could have been a man in disguise.

The support and endorsement of my fledgling TV work by Ed Murrow, Cronkite and those other talented veterans filled me with gratification as I was driven in a company car to Lillian Gish's apartment in the Bronx.

The 61-year-old actress, lively, tiny and pretty, greeted me and my technicians warmly and had coffee and pastries waiting for us. The walls of her spacious flat were covered with pictures of herself, her actress sister Dorothy, and others from her career.

While my cameraman set up and the sound guy got the mics and wiring ready, Miss Gish and I chatted like old friends. She had an open and expressive face. I told her I enjoyed her recent role as the matriarch of the big ranch in *Duel in the Sun*, and she said that working with Lionel Barrymore, Gregory Peck and Joseph Cotten "had inspired these old bones."

In the interview, I approached her relations with D. W. Griffith in the silent days obliquely, merely hinting at whether they'd had an affair. She would only say that she learned a lot about life from Griffith, and I let her coquettish smile speak for itself.

Asked about her brief work with Sennett, she said, "That big Canadian was a sweetheart, and what excellent ideas the man had. Why would anyone ever want to shoot him?" She offered some positive memories about both him and Roach that I could use.

When the interview was over and my guys were packing up their equipment, Miss Gish leaned forward, gazed directly at my eyes with an unsettling intensity as if she could see deep inside me, and said quietly, "Young man, you know who shot Mack."

Was she serious?

"I do?"

"Yes, you do."

THIRTY

We were chasing the sun flying west, so the long flight home got in at 3 p.m., still plenty of daylight left in L.A.

The night before, Walter and Betsy Cronkite had taken me to the musical *Oklahoma* at the City Center Theatre, starring Florence Henderson as Laurey. So nice of them. They'd had an extra ticket because their daughter hadn't been able to go. What a grand way to spend my last night in New York!

In the souvenir shop at Idlewild I bought an inexpensive little model of the Statue of Liberty to give to Valerie. It was kitschy but I'd forgotten to get something nicer in Manhattan.

On the plane I read the rest of *Sweet Thursday*, dozed some, and thought about what Lillian Gish said at the close of yesterday's interview. I was spooked by it. When she gazed directly into my eyes I got the same eerie feeling I'd had when Dr. Edmonds hypnotized me, that she saw something inside me that I should be aware of but wasn't.

For the life of me, I couldn't put my finger on how I might know who shot Mack Sennett.

I stopped by the office to check for messages and ask Miss Morgan if anything had come up that I needed to deal with. She said Bambi had called to say she passed all her finals and would be in on Monday. I was happy about the finals and would have good news for her: the paying job with CBS.

Before leaving, I called Valerie at Lockheed to let her know I was home and would see her soon. But a man answered at her number, and said, "Valerie's away from her desk at the moment, coffee break I think. You must be her hubby, Mr. Weaver. I'm her supervisor, Herb Fuller. It's a shame you weren't available to join our trip to White Sands."

What the hell! "Join your trip?" I asked.

"Right, Spouses were included. My wife very much

enjoyed it."

I said something that I hoped was pleasant and hung up. Went down in the elevator feeling pretty damned upset.

I got home about 4:30, so I unpacked and then thought about dinner. I searched the fridge, didn't see anything that caught my fancy, so I decided to cook up spaghetti. We had some French bread and broccoli I could steam to round out the meal. I wondered if Valerie was aware that I now knew spouses could have gone to New Mexico. Her boss might have mentioned our brief conversation.

When she got home an hour later, she gave me an ardent hug and kiss. "So glad you're home safe and sound, Sailor." Either she didn't know or was doing a great acting job. She tossed her purse on a side table and accepted the glass of pinot noir I offered. I picked up my own glass and we clinked them, Val saying, "Thanks. Me gone last weekend and now you for three days, we have a lot of catching up to do."

"That's for sure," I said, and got right to it. "The first catching up I'd like to do is hear why you told your boss I wasn't available to go to White Sands."

"Oh!" Valerie took a step back and seemed to slump a little. "I see. Dr. Fuller said you called. I guess he spilled the beans."

She stepped forward again and seemed to gather strength. "Well Jake, it's like this. I didn't want to be seen as the little wifey of the big CBS man. Didn't want to be in your shadow. I wanted to meet von Braun and speak to him as a colleague in the rocket industry, not as the handmaiden of the newsman he knew. You've become well known since you got into TV and that's wonderful. But I want to have my own reputation, in rocket science, not be a sideshow. Can you understand that?"

Valerie was saying things I hadn't considered. I'd always regarded our marriage as a partnership, with her beside me, not behind in my shadow. What was I going to say?

I took a sip of wine, buying a few seconds, then came out with, "Valerie, I've never for a moment thought of you as any kind of sideshow to me or my career, but rather as a teammate. I've always admired that you have ambition. I support that." We drew together and kissed. "Thanks," she said. "I needed to hear that."

I felt a little better but not great. Why hadn't she told me all that before the trip to New Mexico? Had she wanted more alone time with that Alex guy, or maybe Dr. Fuller, where they had evenings together, and hotel rooms, away from the factory? Was I getting a little paranoid? Yeah, probably.

She'd seen me go off to Europe on three separate occasions, twice during the war, each time taking huge risks. She couldn't have been sure that I'd even return. I guess I never really considered how hard that must've been on her. Damn, I *should* have. Now for the first time, she got to leave on a trip that was important to her. It was *her* turn, a turn that was way overdue.

"Valerie," I said, "I promise to be more supportive and dialed in on your desires from now on. You have your goals and I want you to achieve them."

"I appreciate you saying that, Jake. It means a lot to me."

Then I got out the tin Statue of Liberty replica and handed it to her, saying, "Here, Sweets, a little something from New York. I should've done better, got you a nice gift from a store in Manhattan but I just ran out of time."

"I like it," she said.

"Liar," I responded.

"No I do, it's cute. I'll put it on my vanity."

"Well, let's get some chow going," I said, heading for the kitchen and the spaghetti I'd gotten out.

Over dinner, I told Valerie about Lillian Gish telling me with an eerie firmness that I knew who shot Mack Sennett and that her words had unnerved me a bit ever since.

"Remarkable," Valerie said. "Maybe Miss Gish is a psychic. I do know that with you still waters run deep."

She put down her fork, sipped some wine, and said softly, "I've had a scary, strange feeling too, Jake. I've woken the last couple of nights with a smothering sense that something bad is going to happen."

On Monday, I told Bambi about her new paying job with CBS and that it would start the Monday after graduation. She leaped at me with a hug and kiss, which I didn't resist; I thought it appropriate under the circumstances. Bambi declared, "Oh thank you, thank you, Jake. I won't let you down. I'll work my little tail off for you and the station both."

I thought hers was not a little tail—she wore tight Capri pants that day—and it didn't need any working off, but I bit my tongue on *that*.

Instead, we got out our Black Dahlia files and notes. One of the assignments I'd given myself was to talk to the *Herald-Express's* Aggie Underwood, because she'd been the first reporter at the murder scene that awful day.

While I was reaching my old friend Aggie at the newspaper, Bambi called the Honolulu police. She wanted to see if they had any record on that Dr. George Hodel, who'd moved there, a drunk driving arrest or parking citation, anything.

Aggie Underwood and I chatted a while, me asking how she was getting along with the new publisher, W.R. Hearst Jr., and about some of my friends on the staff.

When we got around to the Black Dahlia, she said, "It was the most gruesome shit these hard old eyes had ever seen, Jake, and they've seen plenty. As to who did it, I'd lean toward that Dr. Hodel or the dance-hall owner Mark Hansen, whose house she bunked in for a while. I figure she slept with both of them and they got royally pissed off when she jilted them. That's motive, Jake, but it's also just gut feel. Of hard clues, I got none."

Four days later, Valerie and I attended Bambi's graduation at USC. We found our seats among the folding chairs arranged on the grounds at Alumni Memorial Park on that sunny day. The spring grass was lush and the hibiscus healthy and flowering.

The program began with an invocation, followed by the USC Concert Band playing the *Pomp and Circumstance* processional. The keynote address was given by David Sarnoff, board chairman of NBC. When he was introduced, I leaned close and whispered to Valerie, "Boo. He's the competition," to which she murmured, "Shh, now."

Sarnoff, a self-made man and native of Russia, spoke with a bit of accent, his consonants a little thick, even after five decades in the U.S. But he gave an excellent talk.

At last came the time for degrees to be conferred. When Bambi's name was called and she strode across the stage to accept her symbolic diploma, Valerie eyed her closely, as I knew she would. Even in her flowing gown, Bambi looked pretty.

Afterward, the graduate found us in the courtyard, her mother in tow. She skipped up and said, "So glad you could come, Jake," and gave me a little hug—she was too smart to make it a big hug—then said, "And this of course is Valerie." They grasped hands, both hands, in greeting. "You're so lovely," Bambi told Val, who answered, "I was just about to say the same to you, Bambi. I've heard a lot about you. Congratulations, by the way."

Bambi then introduced her mother, Velma, and more hugs and nice-to-meet-you's followed. Velma was attractive too, a generation older version of Bambi with blue eyes and dark blond hair. She said Bambi's brother was working his job at Dairy Queen and couldn't attend.

Valerie told Bambi, "I'm happy about your new job with CBS. I hear you have a lot of promise as a journalist."

"Thanks, Mrs. Weaver. I appreciate that."

"None of that Mrs. Weaver now. Call me Valerie."

I felt a little nervous standing there while these two conversed, so I turned and drew Bambi's mom into conversation. "I hear you're with a law firm, Mrs. Scott."

"It's Miss Burnett. I went back to my maiden name after my divorce, but do call me Velma. Yes, I'm a secretary at Feldman, Moore and Holland, down on Spring Street. I surely appreciate how nice you've been to Bambi."

Overhearing that, Bambi said, "He's a great boss." I wasn't sure but I thought Valerie's smile at that was a little forced.

Neither Valerie nor I felt like cooking, so we picked up a pizza from Casa Bianci, pepperoni and mushrooms, to take home, where I fetched a bottle of Charles Krug zinfandel to go with it.

"I enjoyed the ceremony today," Valerie said, setting plates and silverware on the table. "Bambi's a fine looking young lady, and you know what? She's got a crush on you."

"Oh, now."

"No, she does. It's plain to see." I twisted the

corkscrew and popped open the wine. "That sort of thing's not uncommon, Jake," Valerie went on. "When I had my first job at Ingersoll Rand I learned so much from my boss, who was so patient with me, that I became quite attracted to him."

This was in her hometown of Quincy, Illinois, where she first became a tool designer, a rare job for a woman.

"He was married, but I probably would have put moves on him anyway if my Jim hadn't come along and swept me off my feet."

She was referring to her first husband. "You loved Jim a lot, didn't you, Val?" I said after taking a bite of my pizza.

"Yes, and it crushed me when he was killed in that auto wreck. His friend Ray Dudley tried to get somewhere with me, but I was in deep mourning, plus I didn't really like the guy."

I'd heard Valerie mention that name before, not long ago, but couldn't recall the circumstance.

"I went through quite a nosedive," she went on. "Till I came out here and met you." She put down her wine glass and said, "Reckless, exciting you. I'd never met anybody like you. You saved me, Sailor."

"Aw."

"No, you did. You saved my life. Best thing that ever happened to me. I'm a little jealous of Bambi, I suppose, but I know that's silly, that you'll always be mine."

While those sentiments warmed me and made me feel better about my marriage than I had in a couple of weeks, a speck of something else popped up in the recesses of my mind. Something was lurking there, a fragment of a thought maybe, but I couldn't quite put my finger on it. Was it something about what Lillian Gish had said?

Whatever it was, I wasn't going to let it affect our dinner. "We haven't had pizza in quite a while," Valerie said. "This is dee-lish, and thanks for remembering I like mushrooms."

When we were nearly finished, though, I felt compelled to ask, "Sweets, do you still have a foreboding that something bad's going to happen?"

She nodded and a solemn look shaded her face.

THIRTY-ONE

After graduation weekend, Bambi had lunch with Ilse. My daughter called afterward and said that they hit it off when they'd met at Northcott's, a Pasadena restaurant near the *Star-News*. "I'm sure Bambi and I are going to be friends. She'll make a first-rate journalist. By the way, she thinks a lot of you, *Vati*."

At Columbia Square the next day, Bambi said she'd quickly felt at home with Ilse and that they planned to get together again. Sitting at my desk with coffee in a mug with the CBS Eye on it, she added, "You must be quite a father."

"I try."

"Ilse told me about how you got out of Nazi Germany,

forcing that woman test pilot to fly you at night to Sweden. What stories you two have to tell. That was really brave."

"Oh, not really," I said. "People just do what they have to in certain situations." I didn't ask if she'd heard what Ilse and my friend Kenny Nielsen were up to. Didn't want to look like a snoop.

"Now for starters," I said, "Why don't you go over to KNX, look up News Director Bailey and see what assignments they might have for you today on the radio side. Remember, you're half theirs."

I got a call from Kenny Nielsen in San Diego. The ex-Marine officer turned history teacher said he was coming to L.A. for a teachers conference. It would be held over two days at the Hollywood Roosevelt Hotel beginning Wednesday, so I made plans to meet him there for dinner.

We got together that first night when he had free time in the conference schedule, meeting in the Library Bar before going to the dining room. He was still using a cane after the serious leg injury he suffered in Korea but I thought he was walking better than the last time I saw him. I ordered an Early Times with a splash of water, Kenny a Manhattan.

He asked how I was doing and I told him about my

progress on the documentary and that we still didn't know who shot Mack Sennett or blew up my car. I described my hypnosis session and said the cops and I now thought the shooter could be a man in disguise instead of a woman.

"That car bombing worries the heck out of me," Kenny said. "You need to watch your back. Do you still have that Luger you got in Germany during the war?"

"Yep, it's in a shoebox in my closet."

"Get it out, Jake, and make sure you have ammunition. And get a carry permit. They fire 9 millimeters, don't they?"

"Well, gee, if you really think so," I said, a little surprised. "Haven't looked at that little cannon in quite a while. Now what about you, Kenny? Is the job still going well? And how is Claudia doing?"

He sipped some Manhattan and said, "Still love the job. I find the interaction with the kids invigorating and our principal is a swell guy, real supportive of this novice. Claudia's practice still isn't up to where we'd like it, but it's gaining some traction. That article you made happen in the local paper resulted in four or five new patients. She said to tell you thanks for that."

"She's most welcome. How's she doing emotionally?"

"Most days she's fine, but I worry about her. The trauma of her childhood comes back every now and then. I do all I can to comfort her and bolster her confidence."

I leaned in and gave him what I consider my most earnest look and said, "Look, Kenny, we've been through a lot. Friends since '44 at that MacArthur-Nimitz strategy confab in Hawaii, co-wrote that book that caused a ruckus. Come on now, tell me, what are you and Ilse up to?

He sighed and said, "Okay, Jake, I guess it's time for you to know. Remember Billy Ninetrees, my old pal in the Gyrenes? A guy in one of his old platoons is trying to blackmail him. You see, back on Okinawa in '45 one of Billy's men was killed by friendly fire. Billy was really close by when the incident took place. It was heavy action; they were in a firefight trying to take a ridge. A Private Travis Jordan fired at what he thought was a Jap crawling across a little rim just ahead of them, but actually he was one of ours. It turns out the victim was the son of an important Army general, Everett Willis."

I knew of General Willis. He'd been with Mark Clark in the Italian campaign.

"To cover Private Jordan," Kenny went on, "Ninetrees wrote in his report that it wasn't possible in the frenzy of combat to determine who fired the fatal shot. A lot of friendly fire gets glossed over like that, Jake. It's war."

I didn't see where this was going or what it had to

do with Ilse. "Okay, so . . ." I prompted.

"Apparently Travis Jordan was a racist, never liked Billy, and hated that he was serving under an Indian. So now, years later, consumed by guilt, Jordan suddenly sees a way to whitewash his conscience, make some money, and score points with General Willis. He turns to blackmail. He contacts Billy and says he has proof that he, Lieutenant Ninetrees, was actually the one who shot the general's son, and he will reveal that fact unless Billy comes through with a pile of dough."

"The guy kills a fellow Marine, gets his ass saved by his skipper and now turns against him and wants to screw him?" I exclaimed. "The son of a bitch! I guess not all Marines believe in *semper fi*."

"Ilse saw something about this on the AP wire," Kenny said. "She thought the name Ninetrees sounded familiar and connected it with me. Billy's a great guy, doesn't deserve this, so Ilse and I decided to do something to help. She said this was the kind of thing Nellie Bly would do. So we're digging up dirt on Travis Jordan. We plan to expose the punk as a blackmailing disgrace to the Corps."

I'd just heard quite a tale. Ilse was a rookie reporter, just two years out of college. I took a gulp of whisky, not knowing what to say.

"Ilse didn't want you to know for two reasons. One,

you've got so much other heavy stuff on your plate right now. Two, she wants to surprise you, her editor too, when we succeed. Big feather in her cap. Now please, *please* Jake, you can't let her know I told you."

I was bowled over by all of this. All I could say was, "Wow!" I finished my drink, and signaled the waiter for another. At last I said, "I promise, Kenny, not a word to Ilse or anyone, but how was it that she came to you with this?"

"Well, Ilse was down visiting Claudia, her old college roommate, you know, and she mentioned that wire story in conversation. She recalled my mentioning the name Ninetrees some time or other."

"I see. Well, if there's anything I can do to help," I said, "strictly on the QT, let me know."

Kenny looked at his watch. His free time was slipping away, so instead of going to the dining room, we had sandwiches at the bar, during which time I brought up the pistol Claudia had before saying so long.

Driving away, it occurred to me that Ninetrees could simply tell that kid that if he tries to blame it on him, he'll publicly reveal that he, Jordan, killed the Marine himself.

I also began to wonder if Kenny had been conning me. Now that I thought about it, the story he told was too elaborate. Had he made up that tale to cover what he and Ilse were really doing?

One thing I took seriously, though, was his warning to be extra careful—and armed!

Back home, I pulled that shoebox down from the top shelf of the closet and got out the Luger. Tried to be quiet about it because Valerie was in bed asleep. The little box of 9-millimeter shells was still there, too. I went out to the garage, cleaned and loaded the pistol, then tiptoed back to the bedroom and placed gun and extra cartridges in a dresser drawer.

"What are you doing?" Valerie's voice murmured from the bedcovers.

"Just a little precaution, Sweets. Go back to sleep."

THIRTY-TWO

Since returning from New York I put the finishing touches on my script for the documentary. Film and video footage was assembled, plus still photos. About all that remained to be done was to select a narrator. I had tossed around Orson Welles and Douglas Fairbanks Jr. in my mind but wasn't convinced I wanted either of them. Then I recalled with finger-snapping clarity that Hal Roach had mentioned the actor William Powell. *Yes!* Hal was right. With his dignity and distinguished, resonant voice, Powell would be perfect for the project.

I called the actor's agent, and found that his man had some open time for a couple of months before going to Hawaii to begin filming *Mister Roberts* with Henry Fonda. He would check with Powell and get back to me.

He got back to me that very afternoon and said Powell was interested and would like to meet me. We scheduled an interview at Powell's home in Beverly Hills for the next morning at ten. I liked the way this was moving. Excitedly, I placed the script and documentary outline in a portfolio to bring with me.

So the next day I was parking in front of the actor's elegant Tudor-style home. I was greeted warmly and shown in by an attractive, thirtyish woman in a tennis outfit, Powell's wife, the actress Diana Lewis. "Please come in, Mr. Weaver. Bill is in the study. I'll show you the way." I recalled that Miss Lewis and Powell, despite a big age difference, had been married for quite a while.

I followed the petite woman's white sneakers through a large living room and into a space of similar size lined with bookshelves. Powell rose from an easy chair and extended his hand and intoned, "Hello there, Weaver." In hearing those three exquisitely pronounced words I knew I had my narrator, if he was willing, that is.

"Call me Bill," Powell said, grasping my hand. "Thanks for coming." The hair was grayer and the face more lined than I recalled but he still wore the distinguished little mustache and looked fit for a man of sixty-two.

"Bill it is," I replied, "and I'm Jake."

Miss Lewis brought coffee, tea and cookies and then scurried "to my tennis game."

Soon the actor and I sat perched on a leather sofa, me describing the documentary and showing the outline notes and script I'd laid out in front of us on the coffee table.

I spoke about the old Sennett-Roach rivalry, brought up names like Chaplin and Arbuckle, and today's renewed interest in the silent comedies, thanks to re-releases now showing on TV.

"I have a great interest in those days as well," Powell said, "and this script looks most interesting. By the way, how is Sennett doing? Terrible business, him getting shot."

He was glad to hear that Mack was at home recovering. We digressed to talk a bit about his career and some of his favorite roles. Inquisitive journalist that I was, I forced myself not to quiz him about why he and Jean Harlow never married, although they'd been engaged for three years, or about his marriage to Carole Lombard. Didn't bring up the *Thin Man* series either. This was about my documentary, not the man's history.

Powell scanned the script and after about twenty

minutes said, "I like this. I'll be glad to take it on, if we can do it in the next couple of weeks, because before long I'll be on location in Hawaii."

"Right, your agent told me about *Mister Roberts*," I said. "I haven't seen the play but I've heard it's quite good. I'm sure it'll make a fine film."

"It'll be an honor to work with Hank Fonda and Jimmy Cagney. We'll be three old warhorses. Now then, I guess it's time to talk about money."

"The network has budgeted two thousand for a narrator," I said. "I know that's not much for a man of your—"

"Nonsense. Save your money," Powell said. "This is a lovely project and I'll be delighted to be its voice. I'll do it for a hundred dollars."

"Oh no, that's—"

"A hundred bucks or you can take your script and walk right out of here."

I reached out and shook his hand. "It's a deal, pardner. Many thanks. We'll tape at our studio, Columbia Square. We'll book half a day for it, to be safe. Shall I call your agent to schedule that?"

I left the script with him so he could study it further. I had other copies, of course. It was a satisfied man who aimed his Chevy Bel Air out of the hills that morning.

* * *

The dinner honoring Allan Lockheed took place on Saturday at the Biltmore Hotel's Crystal Ballroom. Valerie wore a sleeveless silk green gown, a favorite of mine and I was in my tux, which I'd had cleaned and pressed. She was about an inch taller than me in heels but I didn't mind.

At the head table I recognized aviation heavyweights Charles Lindbergh, Howard Hughes and Jack Northrop among those seated there along with Mr. Lockheed.

Valerie and I sat at a table-for-four with her boss, Dr. Fuller and his wife. Her other fellow worker, Alex, was somewhere else, which was fine with me. The farther the better.

Fuller said he was to be called Herb and his wife, Dottie. They were an attractive couple, I guessed to be in their late forties, and good conversationalists. We had wine before going to the buffet table.

Fuller showed genuine interest in my work and television news in general. "I very much liked Laurel and Hardy and Charlie Chaplin," he said. "I'll certainly look forward to your documentary."

In turn I inquired about the Viking rockets and about artificial moons. "How high must a rocket go to put something in orbit?" I asked.

"Good question," he said. "We estimate orbital

altitude to be about 75 miles. "The Redstone launch we witnessed last week attained about half of that, so we still have quite a way to go. We're always seeking a better combination of fuel and oxidizer for propellant, you see." Fuller went on to explain some of the benefits of artificial satellites, including enhanced weather forecasting and radio communication.

Soon after we passed through the buffet line and filled our plates, the speeches began. At the mic, Howard Hughes pointed to a large silvery model of a twin-engine monoplane on a nearby pedestal and said, "That, folks, is the Vega, a great triumph for Allan Lockheed in the 1930s. It was not only my personal and favorite aircraft, but also Amelia Earhart's. It was in this plane that Miss Earhart made her solo flight from Honolulu to Oakland, a remarkable achievement for a woman aviator." I was pleased he didn't add that it was also the plane in which she later disappeared in the South Pacific.

"It was the Vega," Hughes continued, "that carried British Prime Minister Chamberlain to Germany on two different occasions before the war to confer with Adolf Hitler." Hughes gestured to Lockheed, seated next to him and led the applause.

After the speeches, a young man approached our table looking rather debonair with a maroon cravat at his neck instead of a bow tie. He had slicked-back dark hair, light brown eyes, and a slender nose. "Hi everyone. You're looking lovely tonight, Valerie," he said with a little bow.

"Jake," said Dr. Fuller, "I don't believe you've met another member of my staff. Say hello to Alex Bridges."

So this was Alex. Man, I would love to have beaten the crap out of this guy. As I stood I warned myself, Now Jake, don't make a scene, that would be a disaster on many levels.

I said, "Howdy, pardner," and extended my hand. It had been years since I was the middleweight champion of the 6th Naval District but I was still proud of being pretty darn strong. I took Alex Bridges' handshake and put my best bone-crushing vise grip into it, squeezing as hard as I could. I smiled at him and saw pain in his eyes. And fear. I could almost imagine phalanges crumbling. When at last I released his hand, he nodded feebly to the others and walked away. After several steps, I saw him slip his right hand into his pocket.

"Pleasant young fellow," I said and took my seat, offering an innocent little smile.

Later, on the drive home, Valerie insisted, "What did you do to him? He looked like he was going to be sick."

THIRTY-THREE

The next day I gave a lot of thought to the question of who shot Sennett. In some inner place, did I really know? Was it Al "Fuzzy" St. John, the Western sidekick who harbored a grudge against Mack, disguised as a woman? Or some person close to Virginia Rappe, the victim of the tragic Fatty Arbuckle affair? Somebody who got hurt financially years ago when the Roach-Sennett rivalry was intense? A diehard Joe McCarthy supporter who tried to kill me but missed his target? My ex-wife Dixie? No, not Dixie, as we'd parted on good terms, at least I'd thought so. Maybe it was somebody I hadn't even considered, someone I was totally clueless about.

I found myself worrying that maybe I'd gone too far with my super-squeeze handshake the night before at the Biltmore. That possibility was confirmed Monday when Valerie got home from work.

"Well, Sailor, Alex Bridges has a splint on the middle finger of his right hand today," she said after shrugging off her coat and setting her purse down. "It's a serious problem when a rocket engineer has trouble writing, jotting down figures, equations and such. The use of our hands is important.

"He says it's a stress fracture he got yesterday throwing a baseball around with a kid from the neighborhood. Claims he didn't catch it right and hurt his hand. But I think Alex may be covering up, that it may have happened earlier, like Saturday night at dinner. What do you think, Jake?" she asked with that knowing look of hers.

I hadn't intended to break a finger, just to send a harsh message. "Sweets, I just couldn't stand the idea of that guy grabbing you and making out. You don't know how bad I wanted to deck the guy. Believe it or not, it took all the will power I could muster to limit myself to that hefty handshake."

"This may surprise you, Sailor, but I'm glad. It

means I'll be doing more at work for a few days, doing some of Alex's as well as my own and scoring points with Dr. Fuller in the process." Val then took me in her arms, kissed me, and added, "Plus, it's good to know how much my man cares."

I had worried that my action might have backfired, aroused sympathy for the guy, driven Valerie toward him. But then I reminded myself that he'd ratted on her, pointed out her math error, got her called on the carpet. So good for Val! She wouldn't forget that. This was a tough cookie I married. She had no reason to be fond of the jerk.

"Shirley Temple and Deanna Durbin," the tough cookie said. I was glad to see our little game hadn't got dumped.

I pondered a moment and then replied, "Yeah, that could work, although Deanna sings a lot better."

On Wednesday morning I sent a network car to collect William Powell and bring him to the studio to record his narration of my documentary. Before we began taping, he said he'd studied the script, liked it a lot, and then showed me a couple of small edits he suggested. "Just two or three places where I believe it would sound more like me and wouldn't at all change the spirit of your work." I looked them over and agreed.

My opus began with the Keystone Kop days and the early rivalry of the Sennett and Roach studios, advanced to the time of Charlie Chaplin and Laurel and Hardy, and concluded with the end of the silent movies and Sennett's demise while Roach went on to the talkies. The matter of Sennett's being shot came in at the end. If we find out who did it before this aired, we'd revise that.

Powell sat in a canvas chair in a sound room with acoustic-treated walls, script in hand and a stand-up mic in front of him. The documentary, film clips, still photos and all, was cued up on a screen. When we rolled it, Powell was to read along in sync. I'd timed it for forty-six minutes, allowing for commercial breaks and station IDs.

As Powell began speaking, I saw Bambi standing quietly in the control room. She was watching with keen interest through the big window, excited to observe a pro at work.

Powell read it to my approval on the first go-through, the richness and clarity of his voice impressive. He kept in perfect synchronization with the film, voice rising and falling as required.

When finished, he insisted on a second take to be sure. Drank a glass of water, rested for a few minutes, and went back to work.

After the session ended, I was completely satisfied and told him so. Embarrassed about it, I handed him a CBS check for one hundred dollars, saying, "I wish you'd accept a lot more."

"No sir, a deal is a deal," he replied. "And I congratulate you on your project. I'm sure the finished product will be a winner. I thanked him again and wished him luck on the film in Hawaii.

After he left, Bambi said, "Thanks for letting me watch. Mr. Powell was really smooth, wasn't he? I was tempted to ask for his autograph but I knew that would be tacky."

It looked as if my protégé was growing up a little.

On Monday I got a call from Detective Owen Wannamaker, who said, "Listen, Weaver, we just got a match for those fingerprints we found below the door panel on your demolished car."

"That's terrific. Whose are they?"

"Somebody named Raymond Dudley. We don't know anything about him, got no previous record, but he was printed when he got hired as a nurse at a local hospital. That's part of the state licensing procedure. We'll keep a close watch on him for a few days before bringing him in for questioning. You want his address?"

I hadn't heard of Raymond Dudley, but I said

sure and jotted it down. After hanging up, I thought, wait, maybe I had heard that name. It sounded a little familiar somehow.

THIRTY-FOUR

I had some Porterhouse steaks ready to broil Monday but Valerie didn't come home at her usual time. Her shift ended at 5 and she usually got here by 5:45 or so, depending on traffic. By 6:30 I started to get worried. At 6:45 I called her number at work but there was no answer.

The radio was on in the background. That's when I heard, "We interrupt this program for a news bulletin. It's been reported that a woman has been abducted in broad daylight in the employee parking lot at the Lockheed plant in Burbank. Witnesses said that a woman was about to unlock her car when a man seized her and pulled her into a different vehicle, one that was parked nearby, and sped away. Burbank Police have been informed and are asking any other possible witnesses to come forward with whatever information they may have."

Right away I knew who it was! It was Valerie and the kidnapper was Alex Bridges. The guy had snapped. It was probably my fault for breaking his finger.

I grabbed our phone book and started searching for an Alex Bridges. Hoped to hell his number was listed. I found eight Bridges with first names starting with an A. There were three Adams, two Allens, one Anthony, one Andrew, and also one Alex! Thank you, God.

I jotted the number and address in my notebook—it was Victoria Avenue—and called the place.

When he answered, I shouted, "Don't you hurt her! Don't harm her in any way! I'll be right there." I hung up before he could say a word.

Grabbing my notebook and my Luger, I bolted out to the car and roared away. Victoria Avenue was just off Crenshaw if I remembered right. Not too far from here. Maybe a mile and a half.

I got there in a matter of minutes, breaking all the speed laws. Parked cars crowded the curb in front of his place so I squealed to a stop two doors down and dashed to the stucco prewar house and tried the door. Locked. I pounded on the damn thing and a moment later Bridges opened up, looking scared as hell. "You! Valerie's husband. What the hell!"

"Where is she?" I shouted.

"Was that you who called?" he said, confusion spread across his face. "What's going on? You look like you're cracking up."

"You've got Valerie here, don't you?"

"Valerie? Here? Hell no. Why would I?"

"Haven't you heard the news? She's been kidnapped. I thought you—"

"I didn't know, man. But she's not here. Come in and see for yourself. It's only my mother and me. We were just finishing dinner."

I rushed in and looked around. Fiftyish woman in the kitchen, hand clutched to her chest in fear. "Sorry, lady," I muttered.

There were two bedrooms, which I charged into and found empty of people. "Well, shit," I said. "Pardon my French, ma'am. My wife's missing. I thought—well hell, turn on the news." I noticed the splint on Bridges' right hand. I could have said I was sorry about that, but I wasn't.

Leaving behind two confused souls, I bolted down the steps. Heading to the car I remembered where I'd heard the name Ray Dudley. He was the guy Valerie had told me about, the guy who made a move on her in Illinois after her husband died. And whom she'd rebuffed. And who recently blew up my car!

Good thing I had my notebook with me, a valuable resource. It was habit. I climbed in, sat in the driver's seat and looked up Dudley's address, which I'd just got from Wannamaker.

Off I went, heading for the Cahuenga Pass. The guy lived in Canoga Park, way the hell out in the San Fernando Valley.

It took quite a while to find the place. The house stood at the end of a block. It wasn't one of the cookie-cutter tract homes that extended down the street. Swarms of those had been slapped up in the valley in the last dozen years or so.

Dudley's place, though, was a prewar, one-story, off-white house with wooden siding, attached garage, asphalt-shingled roof. I parked at the curb next door and crept up to the place, making sure the Luger was tucked under my belt. It was deepening twilight now but I could make out a scraggly lawn, not as well tended as the one next door. I snuck up the driveway and tried to peek in the side windows but the shades were drawn. Same thing with the front window facing the street.

There was nothing to do but just go in. On the little front porch I tried the door. Found it unlocked. Clutching the Luger in my right hand, I slowly pushed the door open with my left. Tiptoed into a murky room. No lamps were lit but some light seeped in from an adjoining room. I stopped and heard nothing but my own breath before taking another step. Felt the hair rising at the back of my neck.

I began to search the place, stepping slowly and cautiously. Off that front room was a small, junky kitchen with a Formica-topped table, four chairs, gas-burning stove and a fridge. A couple of dirty dishes and coffee cups littered the countertop beside the sink.

Next, I found two bedrooms, one apparently unused, and the other with a poorly made bed. In spite of stepping warily and as softly as I could manage, the old floor groaned a little. The Luger was still leading the way. I hadn't heard a single sound besides that floor creaking, but was still chilled with fear.

Leaving the bedrooms, I came to a door that must lead to a basement. Most of these older houses had cellars, unlike the postwar places with their slab floors. I eased open that door and took a step. Did I hear a sound behind me? I stood stock still for a moment before taking another step. Strained my ears—did I hear anything?

Something hard smacked the back of my head. Lightning flashed inside my brain. Pain stabbed. Then nothing. My lights were out.

I had no idea how much time had passed before a groggy, hurtful awareness finally began to seep in. I slowly came to realize I was perched on something, a footlocker or a bench, leaning against a cold wall. My hands and feet were bound and I had the granddaddy of a headache. The walls of this guy's basement consisted of rough cement block.

As my eyes gained more focus, a nightmare scene played out before me. My beautiful Valerie lay on a carpet of canvas, spread-eagled, hand and feet bound. She was completely naked. Her eyes were closed. Was she dead?

"No!" someone bellowed. "No!" It took a moment to realize I was the one who'd screamed. I struggled futilely against my rope bindings.

"Yes," answered a man who stepped into view. "Oh yes." Medium height, unruly brown hair, fortyish, this punk wore denim overalls like a farmer. I spotted surgical tools lying on a white towel on the concrete floor next to Valerie. I was no expert, but among them I recognized a scalpel, forceps, and a stainless-steel hand saw. Sheer, cold terror crawled my spine. I bucked again uselessly against my bindings.

"Feeling a bit down, are we?" he said, lips curling in a sneer. "Don't worry, your wife is alive. For now. She's merely asleep. You see, I used ether."

Ray Dudley took a few steps and stood, his back to Valerie, facing me defiantly.

"This woman should have been mine," he snarled. "When my friend Jim Rivkin died, I wanted to comfort the lovely widow, but she wouldn't have it. I could make her happy, could help her overcome her grief. I asked her to go on dates with me, but she refused. Why wouldn't she have me? There was nothing wrong with me. I was a decent fellow. Was going to be a doctor."

This guy was a fruitcake, a head case. He was bouncing on his feet as he ranted on.

"I was frantic when she moved from Illinois." His monologue growing more crazed by the minute. "Where was she? I asked Valerie's mother but she wouldn't tell me, so I hired a private detective. He found she was working in a defense plant out here in Inglewood. So I moved to L.A. A no-brainer. I had to be near her. I got a job as a nurse at St. Vincent Hospital. You see, I hadn't finished pre-med yet at the U of I. But I couldn't wait. Had to be near Valerie."

"You even followed us to the Smoke House when we had dinner there, didn't you?" I accused.

He didn't answer but ranted on. "How could she ever choose you over me? She ruined my life. So now I will end hers! And after that, yours." More shrill by the second. "First, we shall bisect your wife. You will be my witness. I'm a medical authority, you know. I will do the cut quickly and cleanly between the second and third skeletal vertebrae. Less muscular resistance there, less bleeding."

Jesus, he meant it. He was actually going to slice Valerie in two!

This deranged soul might consider himself a medical expert, but he was not an expert on knots. Sailors were! In Navy training, we learned about every possible kind of knot.

I could see that my hands were tied in front of me by a simple square knot which would be easy to undo—well, if I had the use of my hands it would. But since the knot bound my hands it would be much tougher. Still, I thought I could manage it. If he wasn't watching.

"Oh yes, you shall be my witness," he repeated but then seemed to run out of verbal steam. He turned, knelt down, picked up a glass atomizer and spritzed something on Valerie's face. More ether, I guessed. "Can't have her waking up during the operation, can we?"

While he was doing that I raised my hands to my mouth and went to work on the square knot with my teeth. This guy made a mistake not tying my hands behind me. I gripped the working end of the knot with my teeth and pulled as hard as I could. Then I put the standing end in my teeth, bit down, and pulled on that.

In boot camp I was taught that these two steps should be taken simultaneously and could be accomplished in seconds. Not now. I only had one mouth. Too much time passed. Eventually, though, I managed to get the knot loosened enough that I could slip it off. My hands were free!

Now it should be an easy job to reach down and untie my feet. But it wasn't. My fingers were still numb and tingly. My head throbbed. I was probably concussed. So it was slow and clumsy as I leaned down to free my feet.

I didn't know how long I'd been sitting there tied up like that, my muscles stiffening, so I had no idea how agile I would be. Couldn't worry about that now, though. Had to act.

I lunged forward and tumbled awkwardly onto Dudley's back. We toppled together on the floor close to his pile of tools. He reached out and took hold of a scalpel but I chopped at his arm with the side of my hand. He jerked at the blow and the tool took a little slice out of his radius or ulna, one of those. He dropped the scalpel and screamed. Blood welled onto his overalls.

On my knees, I managed to throw a right jab at his face. For a moment, I was a Navy boxer again. My left hook was a better weapon but I was off balance and in no position to throw the left. It didn't matter. Full of rage, I had enough behind the right to do the job.

His eyes crossed and he fell backward, his head hitting hard on the concrete floor. I crawled to him, took his face in my hands and banged his head against the floor four or five times. I told myself to stop before I killed the guy. If I hadn't already.

I picked up the scalpel, crawled to Valerie and sliced through her bindings, hands first, then feet. She was still out cold, but she murmured something and just slightly moved her head. I found enough rope to tie Dudley's hands to one of the load-bearing posts to which Valerie had been bound. Blood still seeped from his arm. Too bad. Let the bastard bleed.

I had no idea where Valerie's clothes were, so I peeled off my shirt and covered her, at least partially. Her body twitched.

The next few minutes were a blur. I remember going up the stairs, finding the phone, calling the police. Then I tracked down Valerie's clothes in one of the bedroom closets. By the time I got back to the basement with them, she was starting to rouse herself. When she saw me, she cringed, eyes wide as golf balls, and screamed at the sight of this man in an undershirt.

"No, it's okay, Val, it's me, Jake," I coaxed. "It's Jake, Val, you're going to be all right now."

Recognition came slowly but at last she sagged against me. We hugged tightly, her head resting on my shoulder and me stroking her naked, shivering back. After a long minute or two of this, I said, "You'd better throw some clothes on, Sweets, before the police get here."

The next couple of days were filled with explaining things to the cops, initially the first responders from Topanga Division, and then Detective Wannamaker. Police paramedics had wrapped Dudley's arm and head and hauled him off to a hospital under guard. I learned he was badly concussed and had some bleeding in the brain.

I arranged for Valerie to spend two nighta in a hospital with a nurse in the room every second. Brought her home the third day, and the day after that she began sessions with police psychologists and Dr. Charlotte Edmonds, the hypnotist.

My headache throbbed for two more agonizing days. I never did find out what Dudley hit me with. A baseball bat maybe.

An exasperated Wannamaker returned my Luger, found in that cellar, saying, "For God's sake, Weaver, get a carry permit. What am I gonna do with you? By the way, we also found ammonium nitrate and diesel oil down there, so he's good for the car bombing, too."

"I thought you guys were gonna keep a close eye on him," I complained. "I'm in there by myself getting my brains bashed in."

"Hey, we got there within seconds of your call. We couldn't exactly sit on his front lawn all day."

I let it go at that.

The media had a field day. Was the Black Dahlia murder finally solved or was this a copycat? Some newspapers said yes, while others remained unsure. The always sensationalistic *Herald-Express* blazed that Dudley was indeed the Black Dahlia killer. The *Examiner* agreed and said he should be condemned and executed by vivisection. The *Times* wasn't convinced, and urged no rush to judgment.

I took Valerie home on the third day. With a haunted look on her face, which had lost all its color, she said, "I knew something bad was going to happen. I told you." A few flecks of gray now began to show in her raven hair. Though shaken and unsteady physically and emotionally, she continued her therapy sessions. She said Dr. Edmonds, the hypnotist, comforted her the most.

Valerie was so beautiful—and so damaged. I would give anything if I could make her whole again but I knew she would have to do that mostly by herself, to find the strength from within.

Her boss Dr. Fuller told her to take as much time off as she needed. I took a couple of days off myself, a local KNX-TV reporter filling in for me.

On the fourth day I said to Valerie, "Dan Dailey and

Gordon MacRae." She gazed at me blankly as if she had no idea what I was talking about.

She wouldn't sleep with me for the first several nights, said she was terrified of having a man in bed with her, even me. I was patient about that and slept in the guest room.

Valerie said she was having some bad nightmares. My own kept coming back, too. Hers were about naked men chasing her, mine about being shot at.

At breakfast the fifth morning, she said, "I fought him, Jake. I really fought him. I would have killed him if it wasn't for that chloroform or ether or whatever." "You would have, too," I concurred. Couldn't be more proud of her.

Gradually, Valerie began to resemble her old self. She said the therapy sessions were giving her a sense of calm and renewal. Some evenings we just sat quietly, holding hands. After six days, we resumed sleeping together, though we didn't make love. I could tell she wasn't ready for that.

THIRTY-FIVE

So our lives slowly returned to normal. Almost. We both knew we'd never be all the way back to the old normal and that we'd have to make the *new normal* as good as possible.

I was back at work. While the *Times* wasn't convinced that Ray Dudley had murdered Elizabeth Short, Bambi was. "You did it, you captured the Black Dahlia killer!" she insisted.

I shook my head and said, "We don't know that." But I did know this—I had checked: Elizabeth Short had been sliced through the second and third skeletal vertebrae, just as Dudley said he would do to Valerie. That sure gave me pause.

The police didn't know for sure, either. While unable to prove that he was the Black Dahlia killer, Dudley was convicted of two attempted murders plus intent to cause grievous bodily harm. He would be sentenced to twenty years in San Quentin.

Valerie finally returned to work. When she got home the first night, she said, "It felt good to get back in harness. Doc Fuller was swell. I could tell he missed me."

"You'll go far in rocket science," I said, "and your career is every bit as important as mine."

"Oh, thanks, Jake. That means a lot to me. Say, by the way, Alex Bridges is gone. He got a job at General Dynamics in San Diego." She sounded glad about that and I sure as heck was.

One morning, Ilse showed up unexpectedly at the studio. "Surprise, *Vati*," my daughter said. "Can we have coffee? I've something to tell you."

Ilse and I sat at my desk and Betsy Morgan filled CBS mugs for us. "The news will break this afternoon so I wanted to tell you before that happens," Ilse began. "Random House will hold a news conference announcing a new book called *Forgotten*. It deals with war orphans, both in Germany and Okinawa." The word Okinawa got my attention. My friend Kenny was in the middle of that vicious campaign.

"Kenny and I coauthored it," Ilse said. "I saw so many poor beleaguered orphan kids in battered and bombed Berlin, and Kenny saw them by the hundreds whimpering and starving in the ruins of Okinawa. Those poor, terrified children touched our hearts. We talked about this last fall when I was down there visiting Claudia, my old college roomie. One thing led to another and we decided to write about their plight. Kenny said he enjoyed coauthoring a book so much with you, maybe he could do the same with your kid."

I took a drink of coffee, put down my mug and said, "So you're not working on trying to keep Billy Ninetrees from being blackmailed by an ex-Marine from Kenny's outfit?"

"Nope, that was a cock-and-bull story Kenny made up to keep you off the scent. We didn't want to blow our cover till now. Today it all comes out in the open. Kenny's in New York for the news conference."

"Well, congrats, *Schatzi*," I said, "but why aren't you in New York too?"

"I felt it was more important to come here and inform you in person. Didn't want you blindsided. Kenny can handle New York by himself. He's a big boy."

I got up and gave Ilse a hug and with a knowing look, said, "And you and Kenny never—"

"Of course not, *Vati*. Give me some credit. I'd never mess around with one of your closest friends, and Kenny's totally loyal to Claudia."

Bambi breezed into the office at that moment, surprised, and said, "Hey, Ilse, I didn't know you were here." So my daughter shared her news with Bambi before taking her leave and saying, "Love you, *Vati*."

* * *

The Army-McArthur hearings were winding down, basically destroying Joseph McCarthy, the self-appointed Red baiter. He'd been exposed as a fraud and a liar and was washed up in politics. Good riddance to that con-man, I thought.

I produced an editorial saying that was good news and so long to Joe McCarthy. But I also warned that we needed to be on guard against future charlatans who might come along and make incredible claims about external and internal threats to our democratic government that could resonate with gullible Americans. We'd always have to stay alert to possibly even worse McCarthy types.

New York gave the go-ahead and I aired the editorial the night after Ilse's visit.

Something else was brewing in my fertile brain. I'd be taking quite a chance, but for me that was nothing new. First, I asked my newspaper pal Marko Janicek to join me for a drink. He'd become the top reporter for the *Herald-Express* and for old-times' sake I suggested we meet at the Continental, the saloon across the street from the paper.

"Hey, will ya look what the cat drug in," bellowed Shaker the bartender-owner by way of greeting when I sauntered in. "Glad to see the big time hasn't made you forsake your old meeting hall."

"Hell no, pardner, you know I get down here when-ever I can," I replied with a hearty handshake.

"Which of your usuals will it be, the light or the heavy?" Shaker knew me so well. My light was a bottle of Falstaff, the heavy was Early Times with a little water. "ET and a splash," I said.

"The heavy it is, pal. Marko's in the booth over yon-der.

I took a seat across from Janicek, a Serbian-Ameri-can who'd fought with the Army Rangers on D-Day. He'd become a close friend, one with whom I'd trust my life.

After a few moments of updating ourselves on one another—I didn't bring up Ray Dudley—I proceeded to lay out my plan. He thought it was pretty workable and added a refinement or two of his own, as I'd expected he might. They were good ones.

"But you're taking a hell of a risk," he said.

"Yeah, but I've done that before."

We finished our drinks and shook on it.

Next, I cornered KNX's Jerry Dunphy and asked him to announce on air that I would be making a presenta-tion marking the 15th anniversary of Union Station's opening.

On Saturday at noon I planned to present flowers and a plaque to Eve Parkinson, daughter of the station's late architect, Donald Parkinson. His team had used a combination of Mission Revival, Streamline Moderné and Art Deco design elements. The modest ceremony, open to the public, would take place in the grand building's south garden patio.

Standing by while I spoke with Jerry, the ever attentive Bambi said, "You surprise me, Jake. You usually don't want attention paid to yourself."

"Right, normally I don't but trust me, there's a reason. Now please get this to the other stations and the newspapers as well."

"Aye aye, skipper," she said with a mock salute.

I didn't sleep much that night, worrying. Was I out of my mind? Would I be making Valerie a widow?

On Saturday there I was, feeling like a fool, hoping this would work. I stood in front of a jacaranda-shrouded bench in the rail terminal's south patio holding a plaque and a bouquet of long-stemmed roses. At my side, Miss Parkinson and I faced three TV cameras and a handful of reporters. A smattering of onlookers from the public also stood around gawking at us. I tried to study them without being too obvious about it.

Miss Parkinson, a diminutive brunette in her late twenties, wore a tailored blue suit, a matching pillbox hat and high heels. I turned toward her, smiled, and began to say into a stand-up mic, "Miss Parkinson, in recognition of the fifteenth anniversary of this splendid edifice and in gratitude—"

At that instant the "woman" I'd seen shoot Mack Sennett bolted out of the crowd, pistol aimed directly at me. Just before the muzzle flashed I hopped in front of Miss Parkinson.

I flew backward. Felt like I'd been kicked in the chest by a horse. I fell into the woman, knocked her down and we both landed on the walkway in front of the benches.

"Got him!" bellowed the voice of Marko Janicek, who stood there, his strong arms wrapped tightly around the disguised man, his wig now hanging askew. "Somebody call that cop," he barked.

I tried to sit up, finally managed it. A spot on my sternum throbbed.

Looking up at the man firmly enfolded in Marko's big arms, I said, "Hello Everett."

THIRTY-SIX

You should be dead, you bastard!" Everett Hensley bawled.

I turned and helped the badly shaken Eve Parkinson to her feet, steadied her and brushed some dust off her jacket. TV cameras whirred and frightened spectators scattered in wild confusion. There was always a cop on duty at the depot and he rushed in and took over for Marko. Sirens wailed outside as more police began arriving.

"I'm sorry about this, ma'am," I said. "That man, and he *is* a man, is Everett Hensley. He's unhinged. We'll finish this ceremony in private at Columbia Square in a few days if you feel up to it."

"I r-r-recognize him," she said, still quivering. "Didn't

he used to be on TV? But you've been shot," she said, confusion and concern sweeping her face.

"I'm wearing a bullet-proof vest, Miss Parkinson. I guess it stopped the bullet but it still packed a hell of a punch. Hurts like the devil. I'll have a mother of a bruise."

The cop was putting handcuffs on Hensley, who wore a fawn-colored skirt revealing obviously shaved legs and low-heeled women's shoes. I approached him and said, "I'm sorry for you, Everett. You should have gotten some help from a psychiatrist or something."

"Damn you!" he whined. "That job should've been mine and you know it. But there's one thing, though, I didn't mean to hit Sennett that day. Tell him that, will you?"

"Yeah, sure," I said.

Jerry Dunphy had cornered Miss Parkinson, asking her questions while a cameraman was recording. Other cops were pouring into the garden, telling people not to leave, witness statements would be taken.

Beckoning Marko, I went to a corner of the patio. He shielded me from the crowd as I did a little strip tease. Removed my jacket, then tie, shirt, undershirt, and unstrapped the bulky vest. I put it down, examined my sternum where a purplish bruise was already beginning to blossom, and then suited up again. A somewhat misshapen bullet was embedded in the fabric of the vest. The cops would want that for evidence. I had told Valerie to stay home and she'd agreed, not yet a hundred percent recovered from her ordeal and actually in the dark about my plan. I hadn't told her about the chance I'd be taking because I knew she'd be pretty damned upset about it.

Lillian Gish had been right. I had known who shot Mack Sennett. After the knowledge emerged from somewhere deep in my mind last week I'd begun planning how to lay this trap for him.

Thank goodness Hensley hadn't fired at my face. I had gambled that he'd be aiming at the bigger target, my midsection.

The attempted murder of a network correspondent was news and though I hated it, the affair made a media splash for a few days before dying away. Eric Sevareid came out from New York to report on it for us because I couldn't be covering my own story. A guy named Chet Huntley covered it for NBC.

Eve Parkinson declined to have the ceremony resumed at our studio. She was miffed that the whole thing had been contrived, and I couldn't blame her. "What's the big deal about a building turning fifteen years old anyway?" she said.

Detective Wannamaker took over the case and two

days later I was in his office explaining how it all came about. "Pretty clever of you," he said, "but I would never recommend setting myself up as bait like that. You took a hell of a chance."

"Hensley used to be a fine TV newsman," I said, "but he got consumed with the notion that he was cheated out of getting my job at CBS. He turned to the bottle and just went off the rails. If he can be put under psychiatric care, I'd rather not press charges."

"In attempted homicide, it's the state that presses charges," he enlightened me, "but count on it, Hensley will get a full psychiatric exam. He might end up in Patton instead of San Quentin." He was referring to Patton State Hospital, a forensic psychiatric facility in San Bernardino.

My documentary aired on Sunday night two weeks later, coming on right after the Ed Sullivan and Jack Benny shows, a great time slot. I had included the morsel about Mack Sennett regretting his not marrying the love of his life, Mabel Normand. I was on camera only at the end with a tidbit about Mack having been shot by accident and that he was recovering well.

Valerie and I watched in the Columbia Square viewing lounge, along with daughter Ilse, Kenny and Claudia Nielsen, Bambi Scott and her mom Velma Burnett, Marko Janicek, my secretary Betsy Morgan, and several staffers from KNX. I was embarrassed as they applauded when I closed with, "This is Jake Weaver, CBS News, Los Angeles."

When the credits rolled, Bambi's name appeared as a production assistant. She deserved it, having done so much grunt work, but I hadn't clued her in on it. When she saw her name she squealed, jumped like a little girl, and gave me a kiss. Valerie pretended not to mind.

The phone began ringing. Among the callers were the CBS headquarters gang in New York, as well as Sennett and Roach themselves. Those meant the most to me. I was thrilled and gratified as they each gave it a hearty thumbs-up. And I was pleased that Sennett didn't complain about my making public his Mabel Normand lament.

The show received positive reviews in the papers the next day, not just from my ex-employer the *Herald-Express* but the *Examiner* and *Daily News*. The *Times'* story was headlined "Slapstick's Pies Fly One More Time." I even got an attaboy from William Randolph Hearst Jr., with whom I wasn't best buddies, admitting, "I learned a lot, Weaver."

So my documentary was a success.

The next day Bambi hit me with a bolt from the blue. "I have a date tomorrow night with your friend Marko Janicek. We met when the documentary aired. He seems like a nice guy."

Floored as I was, I did the quick math in my head. Marko was 34, Bambi 21. Not great but not bad. She could certainly do worse, and Marko might be good for her. "Right, he is nice," I said. "Have a good time."

Ilse and Kenny Nielsen had written a splendid book instead of fooling around behind closed doors. Valerie and I each had our own autographed copy of *Forgotten*, and both found it to be touching.

Valerie had wanted nothing stronger to drink than tea since her traumatic episode, but one night she said, "Say, let's have some after-dinner brandy, like old times."

I was happy to hear that, so before long we were sitting in the front room with snifters of Philbert Rare Cask. I shared the news about Bambi and Marko dating and Valerie said, "I find that to be hilarious but actually okay. The Lord works in mysterious ways, doesn't he?"

We turned to discussing the book. "They treat each of those kids with great tenderness," Valerie said. "I was moved by Ilse's piece about that poor, bereft little tyke with those big empty eyes sitting all alone among the rubble after a British air raid."

I took a sip of my drink and said, "Haven't come to that yet, Val, but I sure agree about the sensitivity."

I closed my book and said, "We're doing all right, aren't we, Sweets?"

She met my gaze and said, "Slim Pickens and Chill Wills."

"Perfect, Val. Two peas in a pod."

She put her book aside, gave me The Look and said, "You know what, Sailor? I'm feeling a little horny tonight."

■